GETTING OUT THE HARD WAY . . .

Heavy boots on the wooden deck over our heads. Lots of them. A squadron of them. And judging by his tone of voice, Draco was telling them what to do.

Chances were, he'd tell them to use those boots on my head.

We heard them coming down the ladder. "Now what?" I muttered. "The porthole's too small for us . . ." Not one for panicky responses, Andalaya shrugged, locked the door and blocked it with the bunk.

I felt the dark energies course through me, and out along my arm, then into the wall. The wooden planks blurred and shimmied as if viewed through hot air, then began to buckle. Outside the cabin door, the men were shouting; the lock began to give.

Magically imbued with unnatural flexibility, the planks in the bulkhead warped, and bent to the right and left, creaking, making an opening in the wall just big enough for us to squeeze through . . .

KAMUS
OF KADIZHAR

THE BLACK HOLE OF CARCOSA

John Shirley

Based on a character
by Michael Reaves

A Tale of the Darkworld Detective

ST. MARTIN'S PRESS/NEW YORK

KAMUS OF KADIZHAR: THE BLACK HOLE OF CARCOSA

Copyright © 1988 by John Shirley and Michael Reaves
Cover art by Bob Larkin.

Library of Congress Catalog Card Number: 87-063543

ISBN: 0-312-91173-4   Can. ISBN: 0-312-91174-2

Printed in the United States of America

First St. Martin's Press mass market edition / October 1988

10 9 8 7 6 5 4 3 2 1

This is for my agent, Martha Millard
(and when I say this is *for Martha,* I mean it. Blame her.
It's all her fault.)

Special thanks to Ivan Stang and the Subgenius Foundation for the use of J. R. "Bob" Dobbs, Stang, and "The Fightin' Jesus." Anyone wanting to know more about "Bob" should write to Subgenius, POB 140306, Dallas TX, 75214.

I

My new office was coated with dust. Trails left by vermin twisted through the dust, like some kind of prognostication pattern, and there were dead insects specking the window. It smelled like a rodent had died in the walls. It was dim, musty, and cramped.

"It's perfect," I said. "I'll take it."

Gonniff, my new landlord, was a typical dour Mariyadan; as gloomy as the skies of Ja-Lur. He was squat and pallid and he had a nasty cough. Every so often he cursed his sword's scabbard, which kept slipping off his belt. "That chattel of mine oughta know by now how to pick a man's scabbard clasp. Damn her and this sword."

A man should match his home, and Gonniff was a perfect match.

I didn't belong. I wore my old sword—I'd picked it up from the locker in the spaceport—but I also wore outworlder clothes. I was fresh from the Unity spaceport. And, I had a tan. I'd just come from Bronze, a planet under a brilliant sun that was a thousand watts compared to Ja-Lur's flickering seventy-five watt star.

I had walked out of the spaceport, and thereby out of the Unity's civilization; I'd strolled out of a world of clean lines, pristine surfaces, micro-exact engineering, softly humming machinery, precise temperature control, polished bulkheads, designer-sterility, and civilized laws—and into the antiquated seaport Mariyad, in the nation Adelan, on the sorcery-haunted planet Ja-Lur: dark, grimy, ancient, malodorous, raucous, humid, socially medieval, dangerous as a lit cigarette in a gunpowder factory, and, in this season, hot as a witch's cauldron.

It felt good to be home.

Gonniff looked me over. "You want to live here? Strange quarters for an outworlder."

"I'm not an outworlder. I've returned from two years traveling off-planet. I'm Kamus of Kadizhar."

I was hoping for, *"What! The famous detective who helped overthrow the old Darklord?!"* What I got was a blank stare. He'd never heard of me.

And he probably didn't know what a detective was.

"Kadizhar?" he mused. "An island, isn't it? In the Inland Sea?" He rubbed his jowly jaw, then tilted his fez on his bald, age-spotted head.

"Yes. I grew up there. But I worked for years here in Mariyad."

He shrugged. "That doesn't mean you'll survive long this time around. Things have gotten hard, in Adelan, while you were sporting around the galaxy, young man." He thrust out his hand, palm upward. "I'll take the rent in advance."

Alone in my office, I took my phonecub, Dash, from the pocket of my trench coat and sat him on a windowsill. I'd left Dash in the care of a young friend of mine, Buckfinster, the gadabout nephew of the Overlord Staurian. Should have known better. Though he was primed with plenty of wechels—Ja-Lur's basic currency—Buckfinster could be counted on to overlook his responsibilities when it was convenient. And it was nearly always convenient. So now Dash's black fur was patchy, his pointed ears drooped, his two tails hung limply over the sill, and his round silver eyes were dull. "Poor Dash," I murmured, tossing him a sweetmeat. He wolfed it down and sniffed at my hand for more. "Kept forgetting to feed you, did he?

Or was your share ripped off by those expensive High Breed phonecubs of his?''

Dash stretched and opened his mouth as if to answer me—but when his body went limp, his black fur bristled and his eyes grew large with trance, I knew someone was phoning me. "Is this the detractive?" was what came out of Dash's mouth. A prissy male voice, officious and faintly disapproving.

"That's *detective*," I said. I was surprised to get a call already. I'd only just registered with AT&T—Adelan Telepath and Thaumaturgy—and had just sent for a desk for my office. Hardly anyone knew I was on the planet.

"Very well then, *deactive*—"

"No, it's—never mind. What do you want?" I felt a faint ripple of disorientation at using a phonecub for tele-communication. I'd been using technology for phoning for the last two years. On Bronze, for instance, where I'd cracked the Case of the Calculating Crab, I'd used viddyphones. The previous Darklord's mandate against using technology here on the Darkworld had been lifted—but old habits die hard, and the people of Ja-Lur for the most part considered technology to be bad ju-ju. Not to mention culturally pollutive.

The Dark Arts weren't openly approved of in Adelan—they were the province of the Darklord, the man-who-was-more-than-a-man. The Darklord ruled in the South, by virtue of sorcery. Technically, he was not the Overlord of the Northern Kingdoms. But all the kingdoms paid him homage and a "fealty fee," and in certain shadowy respects he was the true ruler of Ja-Lur. . . .

I was talking into Dash as if he were a phone; the voice of a stranger somewhere else in the city was coming out of Dash's mouth. After a moment, it seemed perfectly normal, once again.

The ways of Mariyad grow on you. But then, so will fungus if you don't bathe often enough.

"I am called Dagmar. I'm a Special Administrative Assistant to his Overlordship Staurian. His Overlordship's

3

nephew once told his Overlordship of your talents—apparently you are acquainted with Younglord Buckfinster." His tone managed to faintly convey his disapproval of Buckfinster for keeping such low company. "We have need of your . . ." He sniffed. ". . . services."

"Yeah? *I* have need of seven hundred wechels a fortnight, plus expenses."

"I am authorized to approve a fee of five hundred wechels, in total," Dagmar replied icily.

"I hereby authorize myself to reject any such offer. My fee stands." Truth is, the tough, hard-nosed, uncompromising gumshoe Kamus has a sliding scale, fees charged on ability to pay. For old lady Fenmippet, three years before, I'd charged five wechels and three dechels for spending three days in the scorching Black Desert searching for her kidnapped son Sporad. Found him and brought him home to her, too. Five wechels and three dechels didn't even cover my expenses. But I knew Staurian had enough wechels to choke a forty-ton dragon.

"I'll call you back," Dagmar said stiffly.

He hung up. Which meant that Dash snapped his mouth shut, and then yawned. I tossed him another sweetmeat; he caught it in midair, noshed it up, and purred with a sound like a bell ringing softly in the distance.

It was hot in my office. On Ja-Lur it's said that, though the sun that Ja-Lur orbits seems far away and dim, it's a hot sun out of sheer spite. It was a small sun that grudged light but somehow gave out heat the way an angry sergeant gives orders. Daylight on Ja-Lur—not for nothing nicknamed the Darkworld—was at best a little softer than twilight. And I was wearing a trench coat and a slouch hat. I knew it was too hot for them, but I'd bought them on Earth from a salesman who assured me that centuries before, they'd been worn by Humphrey Bogart in *The Maltese Falcon*.

I needed fresh, cool air. I went to the window and opened it. Took a deep breath. And gagged, nearly lost the synthetic lunch I'd gotten in the spaceport. Someone had

4

just emptied their chamber pot out the next window over and the stuff was oozing down the cracked rain gutter toward me.

I took a step back but continued looking out the window, inspecting the view that went with the new office. I checked out the crenelated stone roofs and age-weathered gargoyles atop the gaunt buildings crowding the Thieves' Maze; the red gonfalons hanging limply, impotent, over WhoreSquare; and below, visible in torchlight, the splotchy awnings of a marketplace all but filled the narrow, crooked, stone-flagged street. The desert turnip salesman, too poor to have an awning over his cart, was just scraping chamber-pot offal from his wares. After a moment he gave up and simply flipped the turnips over. Ah, Mariyad.

I turned and looked around, squinting in the late afternoon murk. I was glad Dagmar was putting me off for now. I wanted time to think about settling in. Certainly no one else would trouble me that day—it was only by strange chance that Staurian needed me. There would be time to—

The door burst open. It had been thrust open by a tongue.

Dash and I looked at the thing in the hallway. Dash squeaked and leaped headfirst into the pocket of my trench coat.

Outside the door was a head. It was a man's head, or more precisely a giant's head the size of a small outbuilding, completely filling the space at the top of the stairs. I could hear the wooden walls creak from its pressure. It was a head, just a head, but it was a head so big that its face filled the open doorway. I could see only one of its brown eyes, big as a bucket, glaring through the door, as its two-meter tongue slipped greasily back into its bear-pit of a mouth. That huge mouth grinned, showing teeth big as ninepins. The teeth were capped. There was a diamond set into one of the incisors. "Kamus of Kadizhar?" A voice like a foghorn.

"No, uh-uh," I said, smiling politely and taking a long step backward. "Wrong house. Wrong office. Wrong guy."

"You are he. You have the Darklander blood in you: I sense it. You are Kamus. I dislike liars, Kamus."

"Oh." I swallowed. "Ah. Um. That's right. It all comes back now. I'm Kamus. Temporary identity crisis. Speaking of identities . . . Who are you?"

The giant's head turned to look through the door with its other eye. As it shifted I could see a nose that would have been fairly aristocratic if it hadn't been as big as a jungle wolf, and an ear that would have made a nice lawn chair. He had arching, slightly plucked eyebrows and a sardonic expression. Despite the half-plucked brows it was definitely a male countenance. Human size, there would have been nothing supernatural, nothing monstrous about this head. Dangling from an earlobe was a huge copper earring shaped like three overlapping scythes, each scythe ending in a glass bead of a separate color; blue, green, and gold. I had seen such an earring before, and eyebrows plucked in just that manner. The earring indicated he was a Charlatan, a supposed magician; the three beads meant he was a Charlatan trained for the entertainment of royalty.

My puzzlement was almost as big as his head. A Charlatan is a fake magician, a maker of fake love potions and improvised fortune tellings. Being a true magician—though a half powered one, since I'm a half breed Darklander—I would know another honest-to-goodness magician when I met him. I would sense the Power.

I sensed power in this being—but not the Darklander sort of magic I knew. It was a flavor of the supernatural that was foreign to me.

"I am the Sorcerer . . . Hojas!" With the saying of his name his voice boomed dramatically and flame curled from his nostrils; his eyes fulminated and his teeth shot sparks.

I almost forgot to mention that the walls shook.

I was supposed to be impressed. So I chose not to be.

"You could have just given me a business card. If you had a hand to give it to me with."

Hojas roared; the wall to my right sundered apart, and a hand proportionate to the giant's head thrust through and picked me up as if I were a phonecub. The fingers tightened about my ribs so I heard them creak. Or thought I did.

"Is that hand enough for you?" Hojas demanded.

"Well, in fact—" I realized my voice was squeaking. I paused to clear my throat. "Yes, yes it is. Okay, I'm impressed. Is that the point of this visit?"

I couldn't reach my potion pouch, but I mentally summoned a few words in the Language of Darkness, and hoped they were the right ones. I took a breath, and spoke them. *"Rh'zin Kghorma Czeck!"*

For a moment I thought that my two years off-world had drained my Darklander sorcery away. Because nothing happened.

But then there was a burst of flame around me, a violet incandescence emanating from me like an aura—and the monstrous hand let loose of me, the giant shouting in pain.

I fell on my duff, swearing as I bruised my tailbone. The giant was blowing on his burnt fingers, pouting like a little boy. "You shouldn't have done that."

"I didn't want to. You wanted to impress me, I'm impressed, but I'm not going to let you make detective jam out of me without a fight."

The giant's scowl became a grin. "I like you, Kamus." His tent-sized hand drew back into the wall—which closed up seamlessly behind it. "So I will not punish you. This time. I want no conflict with Darklanders—and it is for that reason I came to warn you: Stay away from Arrowback Alley—"

"I have no intention of going there."

"—Stay away from the Ziggurat of Zoln."

"No plans to tour the Ziggurat."

"—And stay away from my sister Andalaya."

"Never heard of her. No interest in her."

7

"Stay away, Kamus, or suffer the might of Hojas."

The head began to shrink, like a balloon with the air let out, becoming no bigger than a bushel, no bigger than my own head, no bigger than a pebble, no bigger than a marble . . . then gone. *Pop*, and it vanished into microinfinity.

The door to the hallway slammed itself shut.

I sat down on the sagging wooden floor, a little tired from the incantation, a little shaken—make that a lot shaken—and more than a little bemused.

Also, my ribs hurt.

Hojas' grandiose entrance had taken a lot of power. He was no minor magician. But he was clearly a Charlatan, and an entertainer at that, judging from his earring—a specialist in sleight of hand, vanishing kerchiefs, and birds from sleeves. Darkland sorcerers were never Charlatans—not even for a disguise. It was a matter of pride. Where had Hojas come by this power—and what was its nature? The energy emanating from the manifestation reminded me more of the power crackling around an electrical dynamo than the demonic variety. . . . But demonic he had been.

And I could write a book called "Demons I Have Known." Ja-Lur is at a cusp between the universe ruled by technology, and the Dark Universe, the alternative continuum where magic is more efficacious than mechanics. On Ja-Lur, some of that dark universe emerges like the tip of a black iceberg into the universe that Earth-descended humans know. The Darklanders of Ja-Lur—and only a fraction of Ja-Lur's population had Darklander blood—are in some genetic and spiritual way in affinity with the dark, sorcerous universe. Those schooled in the Language of Darkness can command spirits and Fell Energies of all kinds, providing they have enough Darklander blood in them.

Was I right about Hojas? Perhaps he was Darklander after all. Darkness comes in many shades. . . .

The phonecub climbed out of my jacket and sat on his

8

haunches. His mouth opened roundly and Dagmar's voice said, "Kamus?"

"Well, what of it?" I was not in a good mood.

"You might show a little more respect for your employer. His Overlordship has authorized the piratical fee you requested. You are to come to Staurian's manse, in the Regal Quarter, immediately."

"I'll catch the first cart over." I put Dash in my pocket, adjusted my slouch hat on my head, and unwrapped a stick of imported juicy fruit gum. I popped the gum in my mouth, and headed for the door, half expecting the giant to be outside on the landing. I opened the door. A dour face looked back at me.

It was Gonniff. He thrust a scroll at me. "This is the lease. I forgot to have you sign it, but that's no excuse. You are in violation of it."

"Why?" I asked, though I'd already guessed.

He spoke between clenched teeth. "Giants. Giants in my building. Supernatural manifestations. It clearly states in clause seven, subsection B, that there are to be 'No Supernatural Manifestations on the Premises.' Parts of that creature's body were exposed on all six floors. You're just the top floor—some of the others . . ." He made an expression of disgust. "He was nude, you know." He glared at me. "His male parts were in *my* apartment. My wife saw them and fainted and when she woke up she was in a romantic mood. I hold you responsible for that!"

"Not me!" I said, appalled. I'd seen his wife. "You'll have to deal with her romantic mood alone."

"That's not what I mean. I heard the giant shout your name. Any more supernatural manifestations and I'll have you thrown out. Next thing we'll be having imps and elves in the walls. You know what the exterminator charges for that?" He handed me a quill. "Sign the lease!" (I signed.) "No more giants?"

"No more giants." Next time, I thought, he'd probably come as a dragon.

Gonniff nodded curtly and stomped away down the stairs.

I took a deep breath, then closed the door behind me.

I had a date in the Regal Quarter. A date with a nice fat advance of three hundred and fifty wechels. I needed it: it'd taken an interstellar bite out of my savings to pay the exorbitant starship passage back to Ja-Lur. Thinking about the gold, my mood improved, especially when I considered that the Regal Quarter was nowhere near Arrowback Alley, nowhere near the Ziggurat of Zoln, and I doubt if Staurian knew anyone named Andalaya.

"Let me get this straight," I said, not feeling so well. "You want me to go first to Arrowback Alley, then to the Ziggurat of Zoln—and then to follow someone named Andalaya?"

"All of this, of course, is part of a program with a specific goal," said Dagmar haughtily. "You are to locate this rascal's source of power, and report as to its nature."

We were in the atrium of Staurian's manse. Staurian had a fascination for Earth culture that delved farther back than my mid-twentieth-century fixation. He was into things Roman, and his house was built in what he supposed was the manner of a Roman home. I forbore to mention that in fact he'd built it in the style of a basilica, which was a structure for business and not for living in. On either side stood grand colonnades in imitation alabaster; on the walls, visible between the columns, were mosaics of tile and glass; Dagmar stood under a Roman arch leading into the narthex which in turn led to a nave broken up into living compartments. I knew the place: I'd been here to visit the errant Buckfinster. Dash knew it too—he stuck his head out of my pocket, looked around, and shuddered. He retreated back into the safety of my coat.

Dagmar handed me a bag of gold. "Your excessive fee."

I weighed it in my palm and weighed Dagmar with my

eyes. He was a weasel of a man, with a narrow face and little black eyes, slicked-back short black hair and the expression of a rodent bent on eating cute, fuzzy little baby chicks; like all of Staurian's servants, he was dressed in a white toga and sandals.

"Staurian make you feed him grapes one by one?" I asked.

Dagmar reddened. "I beg your pardon?"

"Listen, I don't think I want this job." With soul-wrenching reluctance, I thrust the bag of gold back to him. "I had a visit from a giant this morning. I don't mean a guy on stilts. I don't mean a guy who does his shopping at the Big And Tall shop. I mean a *giant*. Parts of him materializing here and there around my apartment building. Head big as a coach and four. Did I mention he was a giant? I mean, a *giant*. He said, 'Don't go near Arrowback Alley, don't go near the Ziggurat of Zoln, and don't go near Andalaya.'"

"That would be Hojas. He was trying to scare you."

"He didn't have to try. Showing up did the trick. He knew exactly what you were planning. He knew you were going to hire me and knew what you wanted me to do, and where."

"He has been using his magic to spy on us," Dagmar said, rubbing his paltry chin.

"I can't spy on *him* while he's spying on *me*, Dagmar. Besides, he could crush me like a bug."

"You have powers of your own."

"I'm not at all sure they're adequate to the task, friend."

He scowled. "Is this a ploy to pry more money out of us?"

"Uh-uh. This is good-bye." I turned to go.

"Kamus of Kadizhar!" It wasn't Dagmar's voice. It was a pompous, booming voice—Staurian himself.

I turned back, sighing, with that familiar sinking feeling accompanying the movement. "Yes, your Overlordship?"

Dagmar stood to one side; Staurian was framed in an

arch, wearing a white Roman robe, with one part of it draped over his arm. He wore his hair in ancient Roman ringlets, replete with a fake laurel coronet. He had had his face altered to match an old bust of Julius Caesar; the face didn't quite go with the bulbous body and splayed feet.

Still, I couldn't sneer at his old Earth pretenses. Not while I was wearing my slouch hat and trench coat in hot weather.

"The safety of Mariyad, indeed of all Adelan, is at stake, Kamus," he boomed.

Dagmar looked at me with a faint, smug smile. Just go ahead and try to turn the Overlord down personally, the smile said.

"We have reason to believe this Hojas intends to use his power to enslave all of Ja-Lur. And his power is apparently considerable. It is just one more wild factor in an already insoluble equation."

"On the way from the spaceport I noticed twice as many soldiers as usual outside the garrison," I said. "Because of Hojas—?"

The Overlord shook his head. "We are shoring up our defenses because war is in the offing. For a year and a half there was peace—the new Darklord, Jann-Togah, has kept the peace. He discouraged conflicts between the nations. But that was before Sartoris."

"And who is Sartoris?"

"A rebel Darklander: a Darkland Fundamentalist, who disapproves of the Darklord's policy of permitting modernization. There are now two spaceports, with a third under construction. Here and there, towns are experimenting with . . ." He winced. "Electric lighting." He grimaced. "Hot and cold running water." He scowled. "Air conditioning." He looked horrified: "And . . . television."

Television? I winced, grimaced, scowled, and felt horrified. "I know how Sartoris feels. But it's futile to try to stop it. The planet can't backpedal forever."

"I fear this is so. And the Darklord prizes the scientific knowledge that the new modernization brings. Sartoris be-

12

lieves in a return to the rule of the Dark Spirits. . . . He's begun a magical guerrilla warfare against the Darklord and his forces. And hence—the Darklord is weakened. He cannot control events as he once did in the rest of Ja-Lur. And war is brewing between Hestia and Rool. Hestia is ambitious. Its Overlord, Thuran, would like to take Adelan itself, after Rool. Meanwhile all three nations are beset by the Stinking Hordes—the barbarians from the Nanule Hills. There is chaos on our borders, and a drain of resources within them . . . and there are some who view Hojas as a gift from the Gods, a Savior who will save us all from anarchy by uniting the nations—under his rule!''

Dagmar snorted. "As if a former court Charlatan could rule us! He has no army, no navy, no capitol, and no principles.''

Staurian shrugged. "But he is powerful. Magic still does not work in the spaceports, Kamus—that has not changed . . . except in the case of Hojas! For him, magic works anywhere. He has displayed his might more than once in the spaceport—he caused a spaceship to rise in the air and turn into a giant insect! It grew wings and buzzed away and was never seen again. We are beset from all sides, Kamus—but I can deal with mortal armies. Hojas, now, is a whore of a different cholera. I don't know how to treat his particular disease . . . and his power is growing. As is the number of his followers . . .''

"How did he go from being a powerless court Charlatan to a powerful sorcerer?'' I asked, reaching into my pocket to scratch Dash's head.

"No one knows,'' Dagmar put in, with a nasty impatience in his tone. Glaring at me, too. "That's why we're hiring *you*. Obviously.''

"Why it should be *me* isn't obvious. The problem is magic—you should pick a more experienced magician. And a more powerful one. I'm only a halfblood, and I don't like even that much to get around. Despite the new laws, there's still a lot of prejudice against Darklanders hereabouts. I don't like to use sorcery unless I have to. My specialty is ratiocination and deduction. Also I follow people around. Hojas is too big to follow around."

"The Overlord's nephew recommended you. . . ." Dagmar said, rather distantly, coughing behind his fist.

Staurian made a dismissive gesture. "Come come—you are an idealist, Kamus, and now that you know what's at risk, you'll take the job."

I sighed. I couldn't turn my back on a whole planet. But I hate it when an authority figure is right. "Why Arrowback Alley?"

"Hojas has a sister, Andalaya of Adelan," Dagmar said. "She has been working somewhere in Arrowback Alley for a pimp named Insible. Our information is, she disapproves of Hojas's activities. She believes that he is endangering himself, and she refuses to take part in it. Hence she will not leave her, ah, present occupation to join Hojas in the Ziggurat of Zoln, which he has forcibly taken as his place of residence. Once a week, however, she journeys to the Ziggurat, evidently to plead with Hojas to give up his outsized ambitions. She believes the Darklord will destroy him if he continues. If not for his preoccupation with Sartoris, the Darklord might well have done so . . ."

"Why haven't you had her picked up and questioned?" I asked.

"She will accept no wealth or power from her brother— but she cannot prevent him from protecting her. Any attempt to capture her is magically rebuffed," Dagmar explained.

Staurian came nearer and spoke in a confidential tone. His breath smelled like grapes. "Every week, she vanishes into the Ziggurat, which no others can penetrate. We are unable to learn how she does it . . . But a man of your ability might do it. Might follow her and enter the Ziggurat. And might learn a great deal . . . And tonight, between seven and ten, is when we expect her to go once more to Hojas from the bordello of the pimp Insible. You'll know her by her hair, which is long and golden-red, and by the cloak of midnight blue and silver trim she wears. . . ."

"Hojas would know if I followed her," I pointed out. "A dead detective isn't a very observant one."

"You are a resourceful man," Staurian said. He placed the bag of gold in my hand and slapped me on the shoulder. "I have faith in you."

As I was on my way out of Staurian's manse, laden with gold and a sense of doom, someone whispered to me from the shadows of the apse.

It was Buckfinster, stepping out from behind a column, crooking his finger at me and waggling it, looking around with theatrical furtiveness. He was a foppish, languid-eyed young man with a spiral of blond hair pointing at the ceiling, and a fine dust of gold glitter on his cheekbones; he wore a yellow silk suit with a gold-fiber cummerbund and copper-colored ascot.

"I'd like to have a word with you too, Buckfinster," I said. "Why the hell didn't you feed my phonecub?"

"Dagmar is the house steward, in charge of feeding phonecubs, watchlions, lamp-bats, and vacuum-hounds. But he's awfully cheap with the feed, I'm afraid." He took out a silk kerchief and dabbed delicately at his nose with it. I could smell his cologne. "I believe I'm getting another one of my allergies."

"You don't, by any chance, go about in another outfit at night, maybe slashing Zs onto things and leaving messages signed *Zorro*?" I asked.

"Who, my dear fellow, is Zorro?"

"Never mind. It's just someone on an old cassette I saw on Earth. You see, Don Diego pretended to be—"

"What, my dear fellow, is a cassette?"

"Never mind. What do you want?"

"I heard your conversation with Uncle. I've been eavesdropping."

"As usual."

"My good friend, it's a matter of survival. Every time

15

some supposed crisis in the affairs of state emerges, Uncle Staurian reacts by cutting back on spending. Austerity is his answer to all problems. Lately he's been cutting back on my poor, meager stipend."

"You don't look like your stipend is so poor and meager."

"It is. I have to make do with two servants now."

I shook my head in wonder. "I'll never understand how we got to be friends—we're so different."

"That's the reason, Kamus. Because we are so different. Listen to me: Don't follow up on this Hojas business. My advice is—much as I've missed playing chess with you—that you leave the planet. I'll loan you the starship fare—cruel as the financial burden would be—but leave you must, dear fellow. Hojas is very powerful. And he'll—"

"Crush me like a bug. I know. But I'm obligated to follow through on the investigation." Buckfinster knew me; he knew I'd refuse to back out once I'd taken the down payment, no matter what. Why this exercise in futility?

"A grave error, my friend." For a moment there was something steely in his eyes as he looked at me. Something I'd never seen before. Then the mask dropped again. He stepped back and looked me over. "Judging from the state of your trouser cuffs, you're staying in the Thieves' Maze. Tsk, tsk. And that sword ruins the line of your trench coat. It looks like a confused erection poking it out in back that way."

I straightened my sword up so it rode vertically. "Any other sartorial tips?" I asked dryly.

"Yes. It's too hot for a trench coat and hat, dear fellow."

"I know, I know. But it won't be hot long. It's going to rain tonight."

"How do you know?"

"I can feel it," I said, simply.

16

"Ah, your Darklander blood. I can't persuade you that it's not in your best interests to pursue this investigation?"

"No." And he knew better than to try. What was he up to?

"Well, if you must go, you must." He gave me a facetious genuflection and minced off into the shadows.

I watched him go, suspecting that there was another reason, besides concern for me, that had prompted his warning. Something I couldn't yet imagine . . .

Thoughtfully, I went out into the deepening dusk. The sky rumbled, and a few minutes later it began to rain.

II

It was wet. It was dark. So was I. I was soaked, and my mood was dark as a vampire's heart. I stood there in the murk and the hissing rain, sick of the stakeout, thinking I'd picked the wrong profession.

Come on, Kamus, I told myself, it's just a light rain.

On Darkworld standards, that's how it was. A light rain was falling on Mariyad. A light rain on Mariyad is just a little torrential downpour—not the dumping of an ocean from the sky that came with a *hard* rain. But it was enough to be a monsoon on Earth, and it had maliciously overflowed the stone gutter on the ledge I'd laughably tried to shelter under in the slimy depths of the Thieves' Maze; it'd slithered down the collar of my trench coat and splashed to soak my trouser cuffs. Was probably rusting my sword.

It had taken me a while to locate Insible's bordello. I'd tried the Bureau of Whoremongery first, Licensed Panderer Division, but Insible wasn't listed. Rumor had him working as an unlicensed procurer of girls for the elite of Mariyad, based somewhere in Arrowback Alley, behind a camouflaged front. I'd finally squeezed a description of Insible from a cutpurse who'd first tried to snip my moneypouch and then, when I'd collared him, had tried to cut away more valuable goods.

My plan was to watch the entrance—which was also the

18

exit—to Arrowback Alley, till a woman with golden-red hair and a cloak of midnight blue and silver trim came out. Then, hidden from Hojas by a spell, I would follow her to the secret entrance in the supernaturally sealed Ziggurat of Zoln. It was no use waiting for her at the Ziggurat—it was enormous; there was too much likelihood I might not see her approach.

But I'd waited here an hour and a half, with soaked clothing, aching bones, clattering teeth, and pervasive gloom, and I was beginning to think I needed a new plan.

I'd seen old Zugg, the black marketeer in body parts for medicinal charms, waddle out carrying a nastily bulging leather bag; I'd seen Gonzit the fence, Darv the fence, and Wush the fence; I'd seen three beggars, two loot-laden burglars, Ankh the card shark, and Lovely Lily the pickpocket.

But no Andalaya of Adelan. I was standing with my back to the corner of the Drained Corpse Tavern. The torchlight flickering golden through its glazed windows made auroras dance with silver ghosts in the sheets of rainwater falling from the ledge. I yearned to turn and plunge into the tavern, dive into a cup of steaming mulled wine, and collapse by the fire. But I remained on stakeout, shifting from foot to foot, clutching my armpits, shivering. Annoyed I didn't have enough Darklore to make it stop raining.

And then opportunity knocked. I saw someone enter the dark mouth of Arrowback Alley, and he matched the cutpurse's description of Insible. Wheezing, obese, swaddled in an enormous blue velvet greatcoat, with a dwarf servant running along beside him, sheltering him with a long-handled, lacy umbrella—the dwarf, of course, getting no benefit from the umbrella.

Muscles protesting in harmony with the creaking of my joints, I lurched into the downpour after them, one hand sliding to the hilt of my sword. Entering the Alley was a big risk, but then so was hypothermia.

The precarious structures overlooking Arrowback Alley

19

projected out in hasty annexes and beetling bay windows and gargoyle-clustered eaves, crooked juts providing intermittent shelter from the rain. There were shafts of multicolored light, every so often, downslanting through panes of stained glass. I could see Insible moving ponderously through a patch of emerald and a swatch of wine-red—and then he ducked under the bearded chin of an idol, at a Public Worshipping Station for the god Stasus, Purveyor of Harmony and Wealth.

Melting with professional expertise into a shadowed doorway across the alley from Insible, I watched, frowning, as the moon-faced pimp glanced over his shoulder and then inserted a coin in the stone urn the idol held in its arms for offerings.

I took a stick of imported juicy fruit from my pocket, wrung it out a bit, and popped it into my mouth. Chewing gum helps me think.

Had Insible really stopped on a rainy night like this for a prayer? I doubted he was a pious man.

So I wasn't surprised when I saw him reach up to the left-side spike of the stone god's forked beard, and pull it like a lever. The stone god rolled aside on a hidden turntable, and murky red light streamed out from a stairway that twisted down into the bowels of the city. Thus secreted away, Insible's bordello managed to avoid paying prostitution taxes to the city of Mariyad.

Insible bent to duck into the secret doorway. . . .

"Oh ho," I murmured. "Ah hah, and all that."

I moved across the rain-slick cobbles, drawing my sword, and slipped through the door before it could close, slipping, also, up behind Insible, who became aware of me as a cold steel blade pressed against his throat and an equally cold voice in his ear: "Freeze, fatso, or your head goes bounce-bouncing down the stairs."

He gasped and froze where he was. We were on the landing; the scents of narcosmoke and the giggles of crystal sniffers drifted up the torchlit stone stairwell to us. I ignored the dwarf, assuming he was no threat. Mistake.

20

"Get him, Chewer!" Insible hissed.

The dwarf's snarl made the hair on the back of my neck stand up. Nothing human snarled like that. I looked down at the dwarf, crouched beside his quaking master, and saw for the first time his face as his hood fell away: It was no dwarf. It was a Cannibal Troll, a thing stolen from the Darklands and brought here quite illegally and evidently sorcerously bound to the Procurer. I wondered for a moment how Insible fed the troll—and then the answer came: The troll fed on people who annoy Insible. For the troll was baring its double rows of filed teeth at me, the steaming nostrils of its flattened nose flaring, its catlike eyes burning, as it poised to leap for my throat.

Its leap came with jack-in-the-box suddenness; with an animal's agility and superhuman strength. Its taloned hands clutched at me as I tilted Insible's considerable bulk off center, deflecting the troll from its boss's fat shoulder. It fell backwards down the stairs—but came bounding back up again like something made of rubber, leaping up to us with supernatural ease, and it wasn't likely to fall for the same gag twice. The strength of a Cannibal Troll is the strength of the Darklands.

With my free hand I snatched a squeezebulb from my potion pouch and hoped it was the right one. Insible, maybe figuring if I was going to kill him I'd have done it by now, tried to wrench free, and I had to hit him hard on the back of his head with the pommel of my sword. He went down like a sack of suet just as his snarling pet leapt at my face.

The troll hit me like a catapulted boulder and I went over backwards, as its slathering teeth snapped a centimeter short of my adam's apple—and I squeezed some of the potion powder into its mouth, incanting, *"Indictus cthule N'iah'zuup Mi-yow!"*

The troll was crouched on my chest, snarling and drooling, about to take a bite out of my face—when a funny look came into its own face. It began to change. . . .

This is what was supposed to happen: It was supposed

21

to turn into a cat. A nice little house cat. A kitten. The kind that purrs and rubs its head on your shin.

It did turn into a cat. An Ebon Tiger from the Black Desert. Two hundred pounds of hungry, barb-tusked fury.

My pronunciation of Darklore language sometimes leaves something to be desired.

But, for the moment, the tiger was a little too confused to be antagonistic. It looked at its new, black-and-gray striped paws in bafflement—and I used the opportunity to flip it off my chest, onto its side, leaving its belly exposed to my sword. I ran it through, chanting the words—carefully—that would send its Darkland spirit back where it belonged. Hot blood and red mist erupted from the wound, hissing. The writhing, spitting black tiger sagged, the shape went out of it, and it became an empty fur rug. A classy adornment for Insible's entryway. Maybe I should send him a bill for it.

Insible was waking up, just then, and in no mood to contemplate the fine points of interior decorating. He was holding his head and groaning. I crouched over him, my blade still hot with tiger blood (or was it troll blood?) and showed it to him.

"I can mix your blood with this stuff, Insible, or you can answer some questions. And do not think to call your eunuchs or to lie to me. Remember that your new rug there used to be a troll."

He groaned. "Ask your questions."

"You are no Darklander—how is it that you command the troll?"

"It was given me by Sartoris," Insible said grudgingly. "He gave me command of it in exchange for . . . favors."

"Sartoris looks for backers among ordinary men?" I paused to think it over. "He's planning a long ways ahead. This Sartoris is no fool." I wondered how the Darklord would feel about this information. And where it fit in—or conflicted—with Hojas.

"What do you know of Hojas?" I asked.

"I know nothing of any Hojas," Insible said irritably,

"save that he's said to be a powerful magician who's taken the Ziggurat of Zoln as his home." He put a hand to his head and groaned again. "What a knock you gave me. My heads spins."

It occurred to me that since Insible ran an unlicensed brothel, he had connections with the Kakush, also known as The Brothers Below: the underworld cartel that lived parasitically off every business, legal or otherwise, in the Thieves' Maze and much of Mariyad . . .

"If a Kakush blowgun targets my back, Insible," I said, "my spirit will know who informed the assassin. And you will suffer for it. My Darkland blood will remember. Now—lead me to the girl Andalaya."

My strategy, at this point, was foggy. I had a vague notion I'd pretend to be a customer of Andalaya's but one interested in conversation with a pretty girl, only . . . there are terrible diseases to be caught in the Thieves' Maze. Afterwards I would keep an eye on her till she chose to go to her brother.

Grumbling, Insible led the way down the spiral staircase. The upper walls were cracked and drippy with seepage. It grew drier as we got deeper, but also more riotous. We passed several corridors down which, through gauzy curtains, I glimpsed a number of unspeakable acts taking place. Even some I hadn't tried myself.

A couple of Insible's eunuchs looked at us from the occasional doorway, but I had sheathed my sword, and Insible, fearing magic, said nothing.

In the bottommost corridor, we stopped before an iron-shod wooden door. "She's in there," Insible said, hooking a thumb at the door. I heard pathetic, high-pitched groans from the other side. The girl, I assumed, locked in with some brutish pervert. Stomach curdling in disgust, I muttered, "Open the door."

He shrugged and pulled on the handle, not bothering with the lock. It wasn't locked. The door swung easily open and we stepped into the chamber. Incense stung my eyes as I looked about the opulently furnished boudoir, at

23

the silk curtains and lavish hangings. A large, muscular man with a thick black beard was lying facedown on a white fur rug, moaning in a high-pitched voice as a plump, blond girl of about sixteen whacked his leathery buns with a metal-barbed whip. She sat beside him, whipping him listlessly with one hand, popping expensive-looking chocolates into her mouth with the other, and admiring herself in a mirror-wall.

She wore a sheer silken robe and black leather panties. Her large brown eyes flashed in irritation when she saw us. "Another? Insible, he'd better pay more than this one! And he'll be my last one tonight, I want to take a nap and then go to the theater. Oh and talk to the eunuchs about seeing to it my lunch is *hot* when it's brought to me, will you? And while you're at it, these chocolates are boring. I want sweetmeats from Hestia. These *men* are boring, too." She yawned. "They're so demanding, and always demanding the wrong thing."

Insible turned to me imploringly. "Do take her, won't you? Rescue her, carry her away. All she does is eat, eat, eat. She's ruining her figure, won't be *any* use to me—"

"What did you say about my figure?" the girl demanded, standing and brandishing her whip.

"Rescue her, did you say?" I asked, puzzled.

"Yes! Get her out of my hair! You did come here to rescue her, didn't you? If you'd only said so upstairs we needn't have had any dispute. I would be only too glad to be rid of the little pig. I assumed her father had sent you— he has some stupid idea she's been abducted. She hasn't been—she came to Andalaya looking for work—"

"Wait a minute—isn't this Andalaya?"

"What?" He laughed. "No. This is Dahlia. Didn't you say you wanted Dahlia?"

"Who are you calling a little pig?!" little Dahlia shrieked, like a fishwife with strep throat. She leaped at Insible, laying about him with the whip, so that he ran bleating from the room. She chased him into the hall. Her trick lay moaning blissfully on the cushions.

"Dahlia!" A woman's voice, but with the tone of a commanding officer.

I looked through the doorway. A woman had stepped from a side door into the hallway. She had Dahlia's whip arm by the wrist. She squeezed, and Dahlia whimpered and dropped the whip. "Insible's been awful to me!" Dahlia pouted.

"If you have complaints about him, bring them to me," the woman said crisply, releasing the girl's arm. "He works for me—and he answers to me." She was a tall, handsome woman about my own age, with long thick golden-red hair. She wore an evening cloak—midnight blue and silver trimmed—as if she were about to go out. This, then, was Andalaya. Not one of the bordello's commodities—but its madame. She ran the place.

I stepped back out of sight, clenched my left hand, and murmured, *"Xero Xox Claw Draines Jhim-mwails!"* All the while performing the necessary mental acrobatics, visualizing the proper geometric configurations, marshaling my Power—and lo, my right hand vanished.

I looked down at my right hand, and it wasn't there. Neither was the left—though I was careful to keep it clenched—nor my arm, my legs, nor anything between. I was invisible—both to mortal eyes and to any superhuman vision except the Darklander variety . . . and I felt sure, still, that Hojas was no Darklander. He had not the right sort of magic to perceive me.

I silently reminded myself that the spell required my keeping my left hand continually clenched into a fist—should I open it, my vanishing would vanish. I would become visible.

I stepped breezily into the hall and observed that Andalaya was quite finished upbraiding Dahlia, who had gone sighing back to work.

I followed Andalaya up the stairway and into the street. When the hidden door behind the idol had closed behind me, I stuck my wad of chewing gum on the tip of the stone nose of the god Stasus.

The rain had stopped. The street was empty but for the mist rising from the cobbles, a striking woman with golden-red hair, and an invisible detective who moved as if he were mist himself.

The Ziggurat of Zoln rises tier on tortured tier to a height of five hundred meters; a step-terraced pyramid, carved of great blocks of obsidian. The lower half of each terrace is sculptured into a bas-relief, all the way around, showing the contorted, tormented souls of men and women holding up the blocks supporting the next level of figures, the total representing the Forty Planes of Suffering. In each plane of suffering, Zoln's followers believe, we bear the burden of the spiritual failures committed by those who have gone before us . . . Drooping like streamers of white foam from troughs in each terrace top was the Hanging Fungi of Zoln, its spores planted by Zoln himself, centuries before. It was said that if you looked close enough at the pallid, gnarled stems and fluted pods, you'd see the faces of all who'd betrayed or disappointed Zoln in his lifetime, their souls forever trapped in the ancient growths . . .

Used to be a hot tourist stop. I'd sent a few postcards from there myself.

But it was no longer open to the public. Now, it belonged to Hojas. And standing invisibly on the corner, pausing in my measured pursuit of Andalaya, I could sense the sorcerous energy field around the brooding bulk of the ziggurat. Could, if I concentrated—and squinted—see the flickering violet hemisphere of it enclosing the ziggurat like an overturned fishbowl.

Here and there, down the street, were the moldering bones of Staurian's soldiers, who'd been foolish enough to try to break through to the Ziggurat of Zoln. Foolish enough—or, more likely, under orders from stupid commanding officers.

Andalaya paused to look around, to be sure no one watched her. She looked at me, and through me. The buildings around the ziggurat were derelict temples of forgotten gods, shunned now that Hojas had taken over the ziggurat, not even occupied by vagrants. There was no one to observe her as she continued onward to the trembling verge of the energy field.

I moved up close behind her, so close I had to hold my breath so she wouldn't feel it on the back of her neck, as she drew an arcane charm from her cloak. It was a wrought-silver hawk's talon, a claw holding a cluster of beads: glass beads the color of those on the earring of Hojas.

She touched the silver claw to the ethereal bubble—and I heard a distant pealing, the sonority of astral bells. With that, the violet shimmer parted in an archway just wide enough for Andalaya. And for me, coming along close behind her. After she stepped through, she paused and turned around, sensing someone there.

I almost opened my fist in nervous reaction when I looked into her face, so close to mine. Proud. Austere. Intelligent. But sensuous, and alert. Green eyes like sentient emeralds. Lips like—

Suffice it to say that dames like her don't often walk into my office. Which is probably why she never walked into my office.

She shrugged and strode purposefully up to the ziggurat.

There was a door in the side of the ziggurat, of course, but everyone knew what'd happen to you if you tried to use it. A block of stone would fall on your head, or a trapdoor would open under you, or maybe an iron spike would gut you. Old Zoln liked his booby traps.

28

So I winced when she walked up to the door and knocked on it.

A few moments later, someone opened it, and she went in.

I went with her.

Just inside the door, on the side of the stone walkway, was a slab of red stone carved in the writing of the ancients. It translated itself for my Darklander eyes:

Be you Ware: You Enter the Lane of Lost Souls. Death is the gift of welcome to the uninvited.

Great.

I felt the dark energies the moment we stepped past the carven slab, and I'd have slipped a roll of cash to my bookie on the bet that the Lane of Lost Souls was well named. I knew that tingling, that stirring of my Darklander blood . . . and the hovering worms of black light glimpsed from the corner of my eyes.

There was Darklore here. Unfriendly Darklore.

(Just keep the left fist clenched, I reminded myself, and it's cool.)

An old priest of Zoln led the way, grumbling, his intricately carved ivory walking stick clicking on the stone floor, the dim, torchlit hall echoing to his senile muttering. "First he takes the sacred tomb of Zoln as if it were a hotel penthouse, then he sends me to answer the door like a fucking butler. The hell with this guy, who does he think he is, better not say it too loud, the bastard's powerful . . ."

So Hojas had co-opted the priests of Zoln. Had done a magical corporate takeover here. And the employees weren't happy with the buy-out.

I followed a few strides behind Andalaya and the priest. On the walls, gargoyles carved of a piece with the green-black stone blocks gleamed in the light of the torches they held in their stone hands; the firelight's movement imparted hints of expression and curiosity to their inanimate faces. Anyway, I hoped they were inanimate. I had dealt much with sorcery—but I was never quite at home with the dark side of it.

The old priest's costume was more hideous than the gargoyles. He wore the excised face of his mentor on the back of his head like a grotesque hair net. The face had been cut from the corpse on the eve of the old priest's death and taxidermically preserved. It sagged dolefully, jouncing with his movements, staring back at me . . . Sometimes, its mouth seemed to form soundless words. . . .

I stepped up close to Andalaya as the priest paused at a niche in the wall in which was a man-sized, painted ceramic figure of Stasus, fork-bearded and egg-headed, a brass scales of justice in one hand and a golden lightning bolt in the other. Some of the gold paint was flaking off the lightning bolt. They just don't keep up historical monuments the way they should.

The priest muttered a few ritualistic phrases, and delicately—with what seemed a precisely applied pressure, not too much and not too little—touched one of the plates on the scales.

I expected the idol to pivot as it had in Arrowback Alley. Instead, it vanished, as the flagstone we stood on sank with heart-jittering suddenness into the floor, carrying us swiftly down a shaft into darkness.

I *almost* unclenched my left hand.

What I did do was gag from queasiness, as we stopped, almost as abruptly as we'd started, and both Andalaya and the old priest looked around, frowning.

I held my breath. The old priest shrugged. "Damn poltergeists. Nuisance."

He led us through a low door into a vault with a groined ceiling and guttering torches in blackening wall sconces. Along the walls on both sides were crypts of age-yellowed glass. The mummified corpses in most were in repose—but a few, glimpsed as we hurried past, seemed to have been frozen in positions of desperation, their hands raised to claw at the thick glass lids, their mouths opened in des-sicated screams . . .

If I'd stayed on Earth, I thought, I could have gone into insurance fraud investigation. Not a bad line of work.

"What of these, who seem to have been buried alive?" Andalaya asked the priest.

"Oh, those." The priest sniffed. "They're disgraceful. This is the room of voluntary capitulation to the Ascendancy into the Upper Planes of Suffering. But—" He sighed. "—some who volunteer change their minds at the last moment. And they expected us to let them out! Can you believe it? Really, some people have no sense of pride . . ."

We passed through a series of chambers and stairways, always getting closer to the heart of the ziggurat. The sense of magical energies at work in the background was a palpable thing, as obvious as the smell of blood and feces in a slaughterhouse.

I had to concentrate to keep from reacting physically as the magical energies slithered about me—if I should nervously open that left hand . . .

The closer we got to the center of the ziggurat, the more the energies grew, as if we were approaching an orchestra whose eerie symphony played louder and louder . . .

Supernatural, yes, but there was something wrong with it as a supernatural phenomenon. It was, in the magical sense, like a melody played in an alien key. . . .

At last we passed into the central chamber. The walls were decorated with intricate, ancient paintings of profane sexual rites, the images demurely obscured by the coating of dust that united every surface in the room. I figured this place used the same housekeepers that Gonniff used on my office.

The room was empty but for an unnatural cold broken up by restless currents of burning dampness, and a throne containing a little man: one Hojas Mor, brother of Andalaya and the currently leasing tenant of the Ziggurat of Zoln.

Hojas was a small man brimming with nervous energy. He was almost eight inches shorter than me—no wonder he'd made himself a giant for the visitation. He wore a white robe rather hastily sewn with mystical symbols and carried in his hand a wand, with a rather oversized globe on one end of it. Most of the time the globe was a dull leaden glassy thing, about twenty centimeters in diameter.

The throne was chiseled of volcanic glass. Smoky semi-shapes twisted with a life of their own in its green-glass depths. Also, it looked uncomfortable to sit in. Not exactly ergonomic.

The slender, bony Hojas kept shifting about on it, trying to get comfortable. The throne was too big for him, by several sizes.

"This damn throne needs a seat cushion, Sperb!" Hojas complained.

The old priest—evidently Sperb—shook his head in gloomy disapproval. "That would be a desecration."

"The hell with desecrations," he said, standing. He pointed the wand at the throne and frowned in concentration. Violet scintillants lit the interior of the globe on his wand and grew into a crackle of energies which shivered from the globe to the throne, surrounding and penetrating it. The outlines of the throne became indistinct—and then distinct again, in a new shape. It was now a soft-looking easy chair of imitation leather, leaning back on adjustable metal joints, complete with a footrest . . .

"Behold!" Hojas said portentously. "A La-Z-Boy recliner!"

"What's a Lazyboy recliner?" Andalaya asked.

"An artifact of old Earth which has never been improved on," Hojas said, settling back in the chair with a happy grunt. "Well, it's good to see you, Andalaya. You didn't bring me one of those nice pasta salads you make, by any chance?"

"No. And I'm going to stop visiting you unless you give this foolish thing up. You're going to bring the Darklord down on your head."

"Hear, hear," Sperb muttered. "Sense spoken at last."

"I am committed, my dear." He looked at Sperb. "Leave us, Sperb. And forget your spy-holes, I've plugged them up. Bring me some lunch. There's a Hestian deli down the street, just past the Temple of Butchered Virgins. They do nice sandwiches."

Grumbling, Sperb went out the way he came in. The dead man riding about on Sperb's head stuck a leathery tongue out at me and winked as he passed, but didn't give me away.

Okay. I wasn't completely invisible to *everything*. I'm not a magician at heart, I'm a sleuth.

After Sperb was gone, Hojas said, in a confidential tone to his sister, "I can handle the Darklord. I have all the power I need to do it—right here." He raised the wand meaningfully. "And if I'm wrong and it's not enough, I have other contacts. Our friend Sartoris. And the Outfit . . ."

"The Outfit!" she hissed. "They're a bunch of crooks. Interstellar organized crime!"

"Nonsense. They're just freewheeling businessmen. They're allies. All I have to do for them is . . . well, no matter. Anyway, what are you so high and mighty about? You run a whorehouse."

She raised an eyebrow. "It's a respectable service. I don't sell *myself* there." I was relieved to hear that—and not sure why it mattered to me. "And my girls are protected from disease. They get a nice salary and a pension. We rarely beat them."

"Fine, fine, but it's penny ante, sweetheart. I've got a meeting with the Outfit—"

"Set up by who?"

"Oh, that friend of mine in the import-export business." He smiled. "The one who arranged for me to get this . . ." He looked fondly at the wand. "Anyway, it's this Dreadday at the spaceport, Bay 13, at sunset, if you want to come and see for yourself—"

"No thank you." Her tone was icy. "I won't be a party

33

to your self-destruction, Hojas." She moved to stand beside him; took his hand tenderly between hers. I envied him. "You were a success as a Charlatan, Hojas. You were a popular illusionist. You had no real magic but you had a lot of friends. The children at the courts will miss you—"

He snatched his hand free of hers, stood up, and began to pace, talking all the while.

"I was nothing as a Charlatan—an object of mockery, a walking joke. Now, Andalaya, I will be something important: the man remembered for saving Ja-Lur! War is brewing. Stupid little border disputes, mining rights, trading rights, accusations of spying—and greed in Hestia, a pointless thirst for more land. Each side responding by building up arms, forging destabilizing treaties, displaying their armies and rattling sabers. Stupid little squabbles and stupid little lusts leading to a great conflagration, Andalaya. It's only a matter of time. Rool will call on its alliance with Adelan to protect it from Hestia—Niax will be drawn in . . . And who's behind it, I ask you? Just chance that all these centuries-old disputes flare up all at once?" He shook his head angrily at her. "No! The Darklord must be stopped! And I have the power to do it . . . And to see to it—" He paused, a faraway look creeping into his eyes. "—to see to it that it never happens again."

"How?" she asked. And I echoed her mentally. "You can't magic away the conflict in our souls."

"With unity! I have my followers already. I have a destiny—they can see it and I can, too. It's not accident, Andalaya, that I came by this power . . ." He shook the wand at her. "It's destiny! With my followers and my power, I can take control, and merge the Northern Kingdoms into one peaceful land. And eventually extend that rule to all of Ja-Lur. One government that will not be divided against itself . . ." His eyes had begun to smolder with emotion. The smoldering was duplicated in the globe on his wand, which shimmered, and transformed—becoming a miniature of the world Ja-Lur itself. He looked at it adoringly. Was it adoringly, or covetously? Is there ever a genuine difference? The golden light shining from it reflected in his eyes as he whispered, "Peace through unity . . ."

That's when my phonecub rang.

Okay, so he didn't ring, exactly. He sat up in my left-hand pocket, cleared his throat chimingly, and opened his mouth. A voice came out of Dash's mouth. A familiar voice, much too loud for comfort. "Kamus? Is that you?"

It was Buckfinster. "Kamus, I really have to talk to you . . ."

The others had heard, had turned toward me, and at the same moment I'd automatically thrust my left hand into my jacket to clamp it over Dash's mouth—which meant I'd opened my left fist.

Flash: and there I was, awfully damn visible. I smiled apologetically and tipped my slouch hat to them. "Evening. Awful weather we're having, isn't it? All this rain. Just thought I'd get out of the downpour. Hope you don't mind."

Andalaya was looking at me with astonishment, Hojas with cold fury. "Kamus of Kadizhar! I warned you!"

"Yes, well, this is rather embarrassing. It could have been worse though. One time *I* appeared but my clothes stayed invisible. It was at a wedding, too. Now *that* was embarrassing."

"You're one of the Darklord's agents," Hojas said, his voice that of a judge sentencing a man to death. He pointed his wand at me. The globe on it had returned to its leaden state—but now it crackled with sinister electrical arcs.

Stall him, I thought. *Oh, brilliant suggestion*, was the next thought.

"It seems to me you said you didn't want any trouble with Darklanders," I said, trying to distract him. "And yet you've been plotting against the Head Darklander: the Darklord himself . . ."

"I don't want any trouble before I'm ready for it. My confrontation with the Darklord will come—"

"Sooner than you think," I interrupted. "This plan of yours to unite the planet for peace is childish. The Darklord is a hard man. He won't give in—and you'll find yourself presiding over ashes. If you really have a power to match his, the world will burn when you two go head to head. Peace? No: the ultimate war!"

"Hojas—he's right!" Andalaya told him urgently.

"No! I'll vanquish the Darklord before the conflict between us endangers Ja-Lur. Now I've had enough of your spying, you gutter trash!"

"Spying? I prefer to think of it as surveillance—"

As I spoke I was backing toward the door, conscious that maintaining the invisibility spell had left me fatigued. There wasn't much magic left in me.

Hojas pointed the wand at a group of carvings in the wall—serpents with nastily moronic human faces—that shrugged into animation, coming alive, whipping free of the wall and swimming through the air to me the way sea snakes move through water. I drew my sword and slashed two of them apart, and they fell twisting away, but others, ten feet long and thick as my leg, came on furiously from every side, slithering around my waist, my legs, my neck, shoving their drooling, giggling human faces at mine . . .

My sword arm was quickly entwined and slowly crushed by one of the demon serpents, as I staggered back into the hall.

Weighted and tangled and choking, unable to speak the Language of Darklore now, I slid to my knees in the darkness of the corridor, distantly aware that in the main room just out of sight Andalaya was arguing with Hojas, something about "another pointless killing." She meant me. She was only slightly peeved.

But I'd seen the look in his eyes. A man drunk on a sudden release from his own burdensome sense of insignificance. He wasn't going to change his mind about me.

And then I saw the figure of old Sperb blurring in and

out of my vision as the demonic coils tightened about my throat and chest. The old man stared at me with puzzled curiosity. He held a torch up to my face. I couldn't speak but I mouthed, repeatedly, "Help me and I'll help you!"

He rubbed his chin—then shrugged, and tapped the ethereal snakes with his ivory walking stick, murmuring, *"Dih-toxde-teez'h!"*

The idiot-faced serpents fell away like feather boas, sliding off onto the floor with a rustle. Becoming ash. Gone.

I knelt there, gasping.

"Go," the old priest whispered, "and go quickly. You have correctly perceived that I will do what I can to thwart that overweening shrimp in the sacred throne room—but I can do no more. Now go!"

Nodding mechanically, trying not to wheeze out of fear that Hojas would hear me, I stumbled off into the darkness, and using my Darklander instincts, found my way out of the Ziggurat of Zoln.

Not until I was out, past the barrier, (which holds people out, but keeps no one in) did I reach into my pocket. And find that little Dash was dead, crushed by the serpents of the asshole Hojas.

Now I was really pissed.

IV

The next afternoon, I walked stiffly back into an oasis of intergalactic civilization.

More contrast. Out of the must of antiquity, the layerings of a thousand thousand dissipated lives; out of Mariyad. Into the spaceport.

The sleek towers of the spaceport hotel; beyond them, the towering starships. Other starships hemispherical, cubical, and in shapes defying geometrical definition.

Clean and controlled. Until Hojas came along.

There's no magic in the spaceport. It's the distillation of quotidian life, except for the veneer of glamour imparted by its cachet as the gateway to interstellar travel. Mostly the Unity spaceport is a place of humming lights and immaculate, pearly walkways and silver ramps and changeless vending machines and announcements made in Standard Galactic—announcements in a voice as changeless as the vending machines. "The white zones are for loading and unloading only . . . the white zones are for loading and unloading only . . ."

And everywhere are the uniformed Unity cops.

There are some intriguing proposals on the walls of the men's room, of course. Some of the alien suggestions would tie your private parts in a knot. There's that.

But there's no magic.

The spaceport is a sort of franchise of the rational and

technological, a branch office of the Unity of Planets. Magic doesn't work there.

Just to make sure things hadn't changed, I muttered a spell to try to turn a nearby security cop's pants into a slimefish from the Inland Sea. Nothing. He didn't go hopping away, yelling, clawing at his groin. Disappointing.

I shrugged and walked on, toward Bay 13. Hojas wasn't stupid. I knew he'd changed his plans for meeting his allies. He knew I had been invisibly listening.

But I suspected he hadn't chosen Bay 13 at random. There might be a reason they'd been planning to meet there.

Bay 13 was a hangar for an interplanetary runabout, the small spaceship typical of the Unity's wealthier families, especially prized by spoiled young men and women on their first walkabout, touring the galaxy's highlights. They were sporty, jetlike spaceships that landed on wheels, skidding down a runway. They didn't have a lot of retrorocket power.

I'd always secretly wanted one. Maybe a Corvette, or a Porsche. The convertibles are nice, except that the helmets you need to protect you from micrometeors can be expensive.

The runabout in 13 was a gold and black TransAm. Specifically, a TransAm HyperDrive II, its spade-shaped nose pointed at the wall over my head as I came out into the wide echoey plascrete spaces of the hangar.

A transparent elevator tube extended down from the underside of the flyer. There was a sticker on it; the sulfur yellow of Unity customs control. *Four hundred pounds Radio Transmission Equipment*, according to the sticker, had been registered as *imported goods, for commerce*. And it was registered in the name Buckfinster of the Staurians.

Suddenly the elevator hummed down from the ship. Its door opened, and I was face to face with Buckfinster. He tried not to look too startled. "Hullo, Kamus."

He stepped out of the tube, smiling, one eyebrow arched.

I aimed for that eyebrow. And slugged him hard, once, knocking him on his duff.

"By the Darklord, Kamus, what was that for!"

"That was for nearly getting me killed. That was for Dash. That was for a phonecub-call that came, coincidentally, at the worst possible time. Except that I don't think it was a coincidence. You knew I'd be following the girl."

He stood up cautiously, taking a step back from me, rubbing his eye. It was already swelling. "You don't really believe that, I trust. I had no idea you were in the ziggurat."

When you hit a man and knock him on his ass, he doesn't tell lies so well, afterwards. That's something I've noticed, over the years. Buckfinster wasn't doing a very good job of lying. My hunch had been right. And if I'd been wrong? No problem. The occasional black eye builds character.

Buckfinster fussily drew a tiny hand mirror from the silken sleeve of his gold and silver filigreed matador jacket. He peered at his eye in the mirror, making *Tch* sounds. "Look at that! How am I supposed to attend the Silver Spoon Ball with *that*!"

"You could make up as if it were part of a costume," I suggested.

"Not a bad idea!" he mused.

"I could break a few teeth to make it more realistic," I suggested, raising a fist.

"Thanks anyway."

"Suit yourself. I see you're going into the import business."

He looked sharply at me. "Yes. Well. In a small way."

"It'd better be in a small way, if you're using one of these ships to import the stuff. Almost unheard of, this kind of craft used for cargo. Unusual . . ."

He dabbed at his eye with a lacy kerchief. "It's not cargo, exactly. Just a hobby."

"Is it? Then why didn't you just bring it in as baggage

and declare it that way? I've got a theory: Customs goes easier on you if you're bringing in stuff for 'commerce,' because the Unity is trying to encourage local businesses to market technology. They're trying to modernize the place. Maybe you knew they wouldn't look at it so closely if you made it an import. What is it you don't want them to look closely at, Buckfinster?''

"This is absurd.''

"Radio transmitter parts, it said. That your hobby? You going to be a ham radio operator?''

"A, uh, local radio station. A hobby and a minor business venture. Always wanted to be a deejay like they have on Earth. You know the sort of thing. Stop Forty Countdown, faking bequests, cop stars—''

"That's Top Forty countdown, taking requests, and pop stars.''

"Whatever. Love it. Simply love it.''

"Sure. I was kind of surprised to see the ship is registered to you.''

He looked at the door. "I really have to go—''

"But Staurian would never have bought the ship for you and you don't have the money yourself. You've never done a day's honest work in your life. Whose ship is it really and why don't they want it in their own names?''

"I have no time for your paranoid rantings, Kamus. I should have you arrested for striking me. Because we've been friends, I'll let it pass this time. Good-bye.'' He pushed past me and headed for the door.

"I wonder,'' I said loudly, "if you knew when to make that phonecub-call because I was being watched by Sartoris's spirit-pawns.''

He stopped dead in his tracks. Turned to look at me. "That is not a name to bring up lightly.'' That steely chill in his eyes again. "I advise against it.''

He turned and hurried through the door.

I looked after him, thinking: Sartoris, Hojas, Andalaya, Buckfinster, Staurian, the Outfit, and the Darklord. It was a complex equation.

Where did you put the X and where the equal sign?

*   *   *

Hojas had been planning to meet with the men from the interstellar cartel at Buckfinster's ship. Why? I couldn't break into the ship without setting off twenty alarms and calling down a dozen Unity cops. But the connection between Hojas and Buckfinster was as obvious as a pickpocket with palsy.

The radio equipment—or whatever it was—was still aboard the ship. Otherwise there'd be a Mariyad duty office stamp on the registering paper I'd seen. So that's what the meeting with Hojas and the Outfit and Buckfinster might be about: Hojas, inspecting the goods. Once it arrived on the planet, it had to leave the spaceport through the Mariyad duty office.

What *was* the stuff with the phony label "radio parts"? I had to find out.

So I went to the nearest Unity security office. The office was on the open air concourse between the main spaceport buildings. I wanted to see the head of Unity security for the hangar section of the spaceport. That was the new guy. Susan Sark.

Okay: She's not a guy, technically. But I wouldn't want to fist-fight it out with her. Something about the way she moves—and her cyborgian muscle transplants—told me I'd come out of it looking like a roadkilled sand rat.

I smiled and took off my hat when I went into her office. Humble.

She was about five foot eight, her upper arms looking unnaturally hefty under her uniform. Razor-sharp blue eyes, a mouth that would have been pretty if she hadn't held it pressed into a line. I don't mean to imply she was wasted as a woman. Fact is, she had seven kids and two husbands (polygamy is legal on Ja-Lur).

She grimaced when I came into the little glass-walled office and leaned back in her chair behind her steel desk, cracking her knuckles.

I beamed at her. "Captain Sark! Good to see you. My, you look—"

"Cut the crap, Kamus. Whadya want?"

I took a deep breath. "There's a runabout in Bay 13 owned by Buckfinster of the Staurians. I have reason to believe there's contraband in it. I need—"

"You don't need nothin'," the man behind me said.

I managed not to jump into the air. But I did swallow my gum. I turned, and looked at him calmly. After the first shock I'm better at hiding my startlement than Buckfinster.

The stranger was thin as a blade and just as unyielding: You could see it in his black eyes. He had the spiky hair and nose screw of a Dead Kennedys cultist from Hardcore, the punk planet, but he wore the formal black short-sleeved business suit of an interstellar salesman.

"Nice suit. What is it makes me think it's not what you wear back home on Hardcore?"

He looked at me with a flicker of respect. "You been around."

"This is Mullen Draco," Sark said, "works for Interworld Imports." There was just a faint suggestion of disgust in her voice.

"Interworld Imports. Now where have I heard that name," I said, in a stage mutter. "Seems like it was in a Unity Bureau of Investigation report."

"They got nothing on us," Draco said. "Neither do you, flatfoot."

"Gumshoe. A flatfoot's a cop. She's a flatfoot. No offense, Captain. I'm sure the arches of your feet aren't—"

"Shut up, Kamus," she growled wearily, looking at the plastic sheet Draco slapped down on her desk.

"That's an order from Major Wagstaff. No one touches that ship." Draco was as smug as a transsexual checking into the maternity ward.

She looked at it and nodded resignedly. "It's legit, Kamus. Sorry."

"The Outfit's got friends in high places," I said. "Looks like Buckfinster lost no time calling them up."

"Whadya mean, the Outfit?" Draco said, showing filed teeth in a cold grin. "That an accusation? What I've heard, the Outfit is some kinda interworld organized crime ring. Hey—not me, fella. I sell encyclopedias.''

"Yeah? Like maybe *Famous Hitmen from A to Z*?'' I didn't wait for his snappy comeback. I turned and walked out of the room—and stopped as if I'd walked into a glass pane.

There was a ten-legged Demon hovering over the spaceport, smoking a cigarette.

It was gigantic, big as a circus tent, and shaped like an old earth octopus but with Hojas's head instead of the octopus's central body, and tentacles that held swords as big as a wrecking crane, a cigarette as big as I was—and a giant wand with a globe on it. The Hojas-headed Demon floated about fifty meters up; its shadow fell over the spaceport.

Sark and Draco crowded out of the office to look. I stepped back in and looked over their shoulders. I didn't want Hojas to spot me. With luck—and a few lies from Sperb—he still thought I was dead.

Hojas took a massive hit on his cigarette and blew smoke down at the central concourse. It billowed around us like a killer fog. Sark and Draco began coughing. I held my breath.

Hojas blew the smoke away with an exhalation like a brief hurricane, so that we staggered and groped. Then he laughed with a sound like boulders tumbling down mountainsides and thundered, *"The Darklord has no power here—but magic works for Hojas, yes, even here, little ones! Hojas the Terrible can be a great enemy—or a great friend. Declare me king of Adelan, and I will end war forever! But spurn me and feel my power!"*

With the sound of a celestial scythe, he swung his great swords—and clipped the symbolic Unity tower in two, so that it tipped over at the middle and fell with a ground-shaking crash. *"The only Unity on Ja-Lur will be Hojas Mor's unity!"* He clove a tall, sleek silver spaceship stem to stern with another slash, so that it crashed down with a monstrous clangor. Then he pointed his wand at it—and as if a film had been run backwards, the starship returned

44

to its original form, the two halves joined and upright, seamlessly intact. *"Hojas takes away—but Hojas also gives! Let me give you unity . . . and I will give you a God you can believe in!"*

And then he vanished with a thunderclap that must've been heard as far away as the Dark Tower . . .

"Wow!" Captain Sark said, shaking her head in wonder. "What an *asshole!*"

"Maybe it's just me," I said, "but I like a megalomaniac. They have charisma. Good television presence." I looked at Draco. He was staring up at the now empty sky open-mouthed. He didn't look happy. "I've got this hunch, Draco, that you're wondering if the Outfit made a smart move working with Hojas . . ."

He blinked—then glared at me. "I don't know nothing about the Outfit. Or any Ho-joss. And mind your own damn business."

I grinned. "My hunch was right."

He said, "Stay out of it. Or I'll get you busted. And that word *busted* can mean more'n one thing, pal." He turned and walked away down the concourse, now and then glancing at the sky and shaking his head.

Captain Sark was shaken up, too. She rubbed her forehead and leaned against the door frame, staring at the wreckage of the Unity tower. "Look at that. I can't believe it." She took a deep breath, and started to walk away, toward the tower. Murmuring, "See if anybody's hurt . . ." She paused and turned back to me for a moment. "Do *you* know what's going on?"

"Not yet. I'm working on it."

"You find out, you tell me. Or I'll kick your ass."

I sighed. "Everybody's threatening me. Couldn't you threaten to tear my clothes off limb from limb instead?"

She groaned and walked away from me.

I took out a stick of imported juicy fruit, popped it into my mouth, and chewed it to the proper consistency for some serious rumination. I chewed my gum, watched cops and rescue workers run to the fallen tower, and made up my mind. I decided to check in with the boss behind the boss.

The Darklord.

V

I was looking through a window into Hell.

It had taken me two hours' preparation to open the spatial rupture. I'd had to soldier through the caballistic calculations, to draw the diagrams, to recite the Language of Darklore. I'd contacted and enslaved the intermediate spirit—a sort of ghostly interdimensional phone operator—to locate the Darklord and open the tesseract. And, no less important, I'd had to don the proper fez.

And then, on a blank wall of my office, a window opened, expanding geometrically from a red spot to a large, luminous red pentagonal gap. It was a window not onto the alley on the other side of the wall, but onto the Lower Spiral of the Astral plane, where the Darklord consorted with his ectoplasmic slaves.

To the untutored eye, it was a view of Hell. Soft crimson flames ribboned up and twisted sensuously through doughy layers of sulfurous cloud. The almost skeletal figures of the indigenous spirits, their color mercurial and their eyes dead sockets, rode the flames like ashes riding updrafts. They spiraled round and round, clinging to the flames or straddling through them, dancing up the fires with the clacking movements of string puppets. They followed one another up one side and down the other, tugged into intricate floral patterns woven around the central figure of the composition, he who floated ecstatically in space between two layers of cloud: the Darklord, a black silhouette whose beating heart was visible in his chest as a throbbing wedge of radiant ruby . . . its radiance and the distant rhythmic interplay of ethereal cellos arranging the sticklike spirits around this grim central figure in a weightless ballet of communion . . .

"Some party," I said. "Am I invited?"

The head of the black silhouette turned toward me. *"Kamus?"*

"Long time no see," I said.

"You are amazingly bold to interrupt me during the astral communion. I should strike you dead for it instantly."

"You forget I knew you when you were more or less mortal. It's hard for me to work up the necessary awe. Anyway, I'm just trying to do my job. I've been hired to clear up some things and it means talking to you."

"Very well. I won't kill you. Has it in fact been a long time since you've seen me?"

"A few years."

"Years. I have been much dematerialized, utilizing this plane and the Dimension of Predatious Fertility, the Red and the Green, feeding, accruing strength for the conflict. Time goes on, but in the Between we are not cognizant of its passage; we are aware only of the swell or the diminution of our resources. I have drained these entities nearly dry of spirit. But there are always more."

"You gather strength here," I said, "but in the meantime your affairs in the material world come unraveled, Jann-Togah. You gain something but lose ground. Your enemies can outflank you."

"Indeed? What have you learned, Kamus?"

I hesitated, conscious that I could spark a global conflict by telling the Darklord too much at the wrong moment. I hedged. "Not enough. I came here to get some background from you. Who is Sartoris?"

A rumble from the depths of Hell. The hair rose on the back of my neck. *"He is a traitor. A would-be usurper. And a peasant."*

"A peasant? They're the toughest ones. They've got nothing to lose."

"*All citizens of the Darkland loyal to their Liege are well taken care of. We have no true poverty. Only gradations of simplicity. Do not paint this Sartoris as an idealistic rebel, some revolutionary bent on democracy. He simply wishes to supplant me with himself. He offers his followers dreams of dominion, and a comforting return to ancient times, ancient values. He would make Darkland extend to all the planet, and he would open the floodgates of the Dark Planes so that the Dires and the Harpies live amongst us. He believes this will increase Darkland's power, return Darklanders to Fundamentalist worship of the dark side of Sorcery. But in fact it would enslave us— the Dires and their ilk would overwhelm our control of them, and would become our masters. I have tried to communicate this to Sartoris, but he is pig-headed. He regards me as a Secular Humanist.*"

"Nasty. No wonder you're peeved at him. You've tested his strength?"

"*My forces have tested his only once. We were overconfident, underestimated the size of his following. We were badly hurt. I purposed to reinvigorate here, so as to transfer the power to my armies . . . But it may be that your observation of the flaw in this plan is sound.*"

"Where is he found, this Sartoris?"

"*On the Mordant Plains. Protected by fulsome magics. What has he to do with Hojas? That was the focus of your investigation—*"

"I don't know if he has anything to do with—"

"*STOP.*"

"What?"

"*STOP.*"

I tried to speak again but a paralysis had me in its grip. My own nervous system had turned against me, was working for the Darklord now.

"*You have tried to deceive me. I perceive your thoughts playing like shadows on the wall of your consciousness. I*

48

*see that you were afraid that divulging all that you knew
would cause a war. You will have to accept the risk. I now
perceive what you have perceived. Hojas is collaborating
in some way with Sartoris—and men from off-world. My
enemies conspire with one another against me. They must
not be allowed to proceed with their plans. I go now to
prepare an assault on Sartoris. If the battle consumes the
material world, so be it. It is only one plane. Go and do
not think to lie to me again. You will be monitored.''*

The invisible hand that clenched me now spun me
around and slammed me against the other wall. To someone watching, it would have appeared that I had done this
to myself. In a sense I had. But only because the
Darklord's mystic fingers were at work in my brain.

I slumped to the floor, feeling like a drunk who's had
five casks too many.

The dark hand lifted from me and free will returned. I
wheezed. The window into Hell vanished.

Mariyad is not all labyrinthine slums, hideous temples,
and palatial districts. The Mariyad Chamber of Commerce
penned the following for a pamphlet sent to tourist agen-
cies on other worlds:

"Bored and cash poor? Looking for excitement at an
exciting price? TRY SWINGING MARIYAD!!

"Ancient Ja-Lur—famous for its Salivating Ruins and
the Mudslide of Mundoori—has another side to it. To
those in the know the Ja-Lurian seaport of Mariyad is the
Gay Paree of the outer spiral of the galaxy. Ask them
where the action is and they'll give you a wink and whis-
per, 'Mariyad!' The cafés, the exotic red-light district, the
exotic lavender-light district, the blood-exchange stalls,
the negative tanning resorts, the legless dancers in Mariyad's numerous exotic nightclubs—and all of it in the
soothing purple twilight of Ja-Lur! The exchange rate is
flexible and generous, and special arrangements for soul-
barter can be made for those whose Unity credit accounts
are a little anemic. Make Mariyad your home away from

home . . . but watch out—the magic of Ja-Lur may capture your heart!''

The pamphlet failed to mention that some people had had to go to the Unity embassy to have their hearts returned to them.

Still, there was some truth to their claims. Mariyad had some nice cafés. One of them is the Cafe Purgatorio, in the museum district, on Giant's Skull. Giant's Skull is a hill—some say there's a real giant's skull underneath the soil—overlooking the Bay of Baldaz.

I sat on the terrace in the soothing purple twilight, wishing I had a watch to look at while waiting for Andalaya.

She was called Andalaya of Adelan because in her younger years, when her features were softer, she'd won a beauty contest locally: she was Miss Adelan, and was the official Adelanian representative for the Miss Northern Kingdoms pageant. The Miss Northern Kingdoms winner was never determined. A disgruntled sorcerer whose daughter had lost out to someone else for Miss Niax caused the judges to turn into flogens—creatures very like Earthly swine—and magicked a rain of slimefrog tadpoles on the contestants.

I was seated beside the stone rail of the terrace, sipping what passes for coffee locally, when Andalaya strode up, with the confidence of a woman used to being in charge. She sat down, after looking around to be sure no one was sitting close enough to listen in on us. It was a balmy late afternoon; she was wearing a tight-fitting green gown, with various slits in it showing enough cleavage and thigh to arouse an army satiated from a week of rapine. She tugged her glove off, finger by finger, then tapped her long nails on the table. A waiter was instantly at our elbow. "Hestian wine," she said. "Make it the blue, from the season of the witch, and make it chilled."

Stuttering salaams to her, the waiter backed away, stumbled over a chair, and found his way to the kitchen. "You have that effect on all men?" I asked her.

"Not you, apparently."

"Don't misjudge me by my cool exterior," I said.

"What do you want? Why arrange this meeting with me?"

I began, "Maybe we'd better wait—"

"Till I'm softened up with drink? It doesn't work. I don't soften up. With drink."

"No? What does it for you?"

"Did you bring me here so you could ask impudent questions?"

"Yeah, but not that one. Look, I know you don't want your brother to go head to head with the Darklord. Jann-Togah is just not a guy you lock horns with."

I shut my trap for a while as the waiter returned with her drink. He made cow eyes at her and stumbled away. She sipped her wine and looked at me expectantly.

"Hojas can't take over the planet," I said, "even in a good cause. Maybe especially then. The people he's collaborating with will wait till the right moment—supposing he survives the Darklord—and stab him in the back. Both the Outfit and Sartoris want the planet under their control, for their reasons. If we help each other, I can save your brother's life."

"Doubtless you're right about his so-called allies. I am not going to help Hojas in his folly—but I'm not going to give aid and comfort to his enemies either. And you are clearly his enemy."

She looked into my eyes. I looked into hers.

I didn't lean over and take her hand, draw her close, and kiss her. I also didn't leap over the table, pick her up in my arms, and carry her to the nearest inn.

But it was an effort.

I managed to say, "I'm not your enemy. I'm a private eye—a disinterested party hired to investigate and to smooth things over. Your brother nearly killed me. I'm not the guy with the hostility problem around here. If you want—we could go to a mindsharer."

She drew back a little in her chair. "That would be—rather intimate. You are a stranger."

"I suggest we put aside the embarrassment for the sake of your brother. And the peace on Ja-Lur." I pointed at the docks. "Look. You see them?" We both looked at the harbor. Above the rooftops we could see the long row of serpent-carved masts of the Adelanian warships, their pennants fluttering in the wind, bloodred against the purple expanse of the Bay of Baldaz. "Half of those ships are new. They're being outfitted for war. I did a psychic fingerprint trace to find that origins of that war—"

"Psychic fingerprints?"

"A manner of speaking. A sort of ethereal trail left by psychic influences. I traced it back from Krah-Mega, the general of Hestia, to Sartoris. Hojas's ally Sartoris has used Darklander power to bend the minds of Krah-Mega and the others to his will. He wants the Northern Kingdoms at war—they are unable then to help the Darklord against him. They cannot pay tribute, and they cannot aid him in other ways. And it draws Hojas, too, into Sartoris's web. He is being used—and there is no time to waste. The Darklord will implement a preemptive strike against Sartoris within a few days. He'll go after your brother as an ally of Sartoris."

Her eyes widened. After a moment she said, "I must know if this is true. Let us go to a mindsharer."

The place was as gloomy as a widow who's found out her husband cashed in his life insurance to buy a necklace for his mistress.

It was dark, dank, and malodorous. But atmospheric, according to the Mariyad tourist pamphlet. "In a mood for adventure? Try one of Ja-Lur's exotic mindsharers, just twenty miles south of Mariyad—where magic is legal! There's nothing more atmospheric than a mindsharer's hovel—"

That's one way of putting it. We tried not to inhale too deeply and sat in the wicker chairs to either side of the rickety wooden table in the dim, earthen-floored hut.

The only light was from a five-candled corpse's hand,

flame-tipped fingers pointing at the roof, sconced in an old cracked cup between us and the harridan. Mindsharers tend to seclusion and slatternly ways, as if the cloak of grime helps keep the unwanted telepathic transmissions out.

We could not see her face; like most of her Guild she'd combed her greasy gray hair down over it; despite the warmth of the close little room she huddled on her stool under a multiple thickness of colorless shawls and burlap rags, a bundle in the darkness. Most mindsharers work for AT&T, of course, connecting phonecub calls, and are constantly grumbling about having to bathe to go to work.

"I am a mindsharer," she said in a crow's voice, swaying from side to side. "I am the channel, the reflective surface, the living wire. I hear all thoughts save my own. I hear now the spiders in the walls thinking thoughts like rusty needles about living food; I hear the birds on the roof thinking of mating with thoughts like stabbing flutters. I hear—"

"Cut the tourist recitation," I said. "My clothes are misleading. I'm not an outworlder." I told Andalaya, "The tourist bureau writes that stuff for them."

"If she's a mindsharer, she should *know* that you're not a tourist," said Andalaya, who had never been to a mindsharer.

"She's wearing a charm on her chest that deflects our thoughts. It works in a limited way. Keeps them from going crazy. They still pick up too much."

Some say that mindsharers are the result of mutants crossed with Darklanders. Some say politicians are the result of ticks crossed with swine. I could go for both theories.

"You want psychological insight, telepathic communion, orgone energy enhancement for sexual exaltation, or what?" The mindsharer asked, now in an ordinary voice. She paused to sip soda pop from a can. One end of the straw disappeared into her screen of hair. "I haven't got all day."

53

"Telepathic communion with the emphasis on truth-finding," I said.

Andalaya shifted nervously on her seat. She was anxious about this. So was I. Not all my thoughts about her had been pristine.

I slapped five gold coins down on the table.

"I can't change that," the mindsharer said.

"Don't have to. The extra is for your silence. You're going to encounter some things best not—"

"Yeah, yeah, everybody says that. We're completely confidential." She pointed at the certificate on the wall. "Licensed, see? Confidentiality guaranteed. And I got a ninety-two on the civil service test." She scooped the money up with a grimy claw, dumped it in some wen of her garments. She reached into her noisome recesses and removed a pendant shaped like a miniature satellite dish on a leather thong and hung it on a wall peg behind her. Then she took our hands, one in each of hers. I held Andalaya's free hand with my own. The circuit was complete.

"You know the routine, know-it-all?" the mindsharer asked me.

"Yeah. I'll focus for the guiding."

I closed my eyes and it began almost immediately. First a sensation like a series of hot flashes, making me shudder though it was almost pleasurable. And then the imagery, the words, the babbling, as if somebody had projected a movie on the back of my eyelids—a movie edited by a psychotic drunk. The visions came with a sort of surfside rhythm, splashing in and then drawing back like waves in a tidal pool carrying the bright fish of the mind to me and away from me . . . fragmentary images from Andalaya's mind; shots of activity at the bordello, viewed in passing, like the activity in a cage seen by a zookeeper walking by; memories: Andalaya and Hojas as children playing on the beach; a ten-year-old Hojas making a seashell seem to disappear.

A babble of voices, Andalaya's, someone I knew was her mother, Hojas at various ages. More recent imagery.

The ziggurat. Kamus at the café. A moment of speculation as to the size of Kamus's—

"I thought the idea was for me to see into *your* mind?" Andalaya said aloud, shattering the stream of images just as it was getting interesting.

I focused, ordering my thoughts and recollections starting with the day my investigation began, my encounters with Staurian, Buckfinster, the Outfit, the Darklord. I tried to head off my personal thoughts about Andalaya but thoughts flow one into another like waves on a stream, the stream of consciousness, all of a piece, and unavoidably she glimpsed my thoughts about her at the café—and for a moment her startlement caused our thoughts to whirl together like an eddy, spiraling with one another, our mutual attraction laid bare (I caught her thinking: *No! Eight years without a man was the smartest thing I ever did—stupid to break celibacy, to admit complications into an ordered life . . . stupid, but—*), her gender calling to mine in the language of bioelectricity.

She drew her hands away from us, breaking the connection. The picture faded. My erection remained.

"You two oughta get married," the mindsharer remarked.

"Shut up!" Andalaya and I said, simultaneously.

"You were telling the truth," she said. "I only wish I could persuade Hojas to try mindsharing with you. But he would never risk so close a psychic contact with a supposed enemy."

Andalaya and I were walking up the path from the mindsharer's hovel, through a copse of feather trees. It was sunset. Pleasantly balmy. Somewhere a Ja-Lurian furdove cooed. The light caressed the soft foliage of the trees with sultry crimson. The grassy rolling land, golden and luxuriant, seemed sensually curvaceous. We hadn't shaken the effects of the mindsharing, yet. In fact, I had a sharp sense that her remark about Hojas was a conscious effort on her part to force us back to practical concerns. There was some lingering telepathic charge between us—a charge that flared into arousal when she stumbled a little over a rut and I took her arm—purely by reflex—to steady her, and the heightened orgone electricity crackled through the touch, and I saw desire in her eyes more clearly than their color, and she opened up to me like a tulip to the sun. We tumbled into the soft grass, rolling away from a vague guiltiness hovering in the background, the guilt of thinking we were pressed for time, ought to be doing something to stop the coming confrontation between Hojas, Sartoris, and the Darklord . . . but this interpersonal explosion simply took precedence over everything else. There was no past, no future, there was only the absolute necessity of joining. Now. Her gown fell away with impossible effortlessness, and her breasts tumbled free, and I groaned with their pale, sweetly freckled, pink-tipped divinity. Her hands were working on me, and I was free of my pants and suddenly sinking into her, all my sensations lost in my sex for a moment, feeling like a traveler who's stumbled into a soft warm wet cleft in the ground, slid into it as if it were quicksand, completely engulfed and not caring: discovering an exquisite loss of self there . . .

And then I was exploring her, and giving, and giving and taking . . .

Thirty feet away two aging tourists from Earth were making their way down the path. I was distantly and indifferently aware that they had seen us in the last burst of light from sunset. "I wonder," the old woman said to her husband, "where we get some of whatever they've taken?"

"We ought to be ashamed," Andalaya said, "putting our mission aside for this . . . this . . ."

"Yeah," I said.

"We ought to get up and concentrate on business," she said.

"Yeah," I said.

56

"My brother needs my help," she said.

"Yeah," I said.

"The planet needs our help," she said.

"Yeah," I said.

"But I think I'm in love with you," she said.

"Oh, *yeah*," I said.

We said a great deal after that, but none of it in words.

VI

"You're failing in your mission, Kamus," Dagmar said. "Your first priority is to identify the source of Hojas's power. It's obvious he's no ordinary sorcerer. You may now recite a list of your excuses for failure."

"Having to deal with assholes like you is probably at the top of my list," I said.

"Cease this impudence or I'll have you fired! Now see here—you've made contact with this woman Andalaya?"

"In a manner of speaking."

"Well—have you simply asked her? She might know how he does it. I realize that your semicriminal brain may not have apprehended this obvious fact—"

"Yeah, I asked her. She doesn't know what the actual nature of the power is. He's kept it from her in case—well, in case someone like me gets close to her. She really doesn't know. She knows he didn't use to have it—it's something he acquired somehow . . . through Buckfinster!"

"What?!"

I told him about Buckfinster's connection to Hojas, and the interplanetary crime cartel, the Outfit. ". . . And Andalaya says that the shipment is being used to enhance Hojas's power, somehow. It was registered as electronic parts. Perhaps it's an amplification device of some kind . . ."

"Amplification? This is disastrous!"

58

"It's only speculation. She heard him say it would increase his power in some way . . . but in what way she's not sure. She knows only that the power is in the globe attached to the wand—which came to him through Buckfinster."

"Indeed. Buckfinster. Most distressing. Since Buckfinster has disappeared."

"Disappeared?"

"Are you a mimic bird? Yes, Kamus—he's gone. We can't find him anywhere. He's taken everything he owns of value with him and vanished . . . Kamus, I find it hard to believe Buckfinster was the source of such power."

"He's got some kind of little import-export business on the side. I figure he brought whatever is in that globe from off-world . . . Hojas used to work as a court Charlatan for Staurian?"

"Yes, for parties and the like. He had plenty of contact with Buckfinster . . . This is all most intriguing—but it does not change the basic fact: You have failed. I insist that you present me with a full report, ten pages single spaced—"

"Stop bothering me," I said. "I'm working."

I pulled the phonecub's tail. With this particular breed, tail-pulling makes it break the connection. The phonecub bit me. It was a new phonecub and didn't know me too well, and I'd pulled its tail a little too hard.

I bandaged my finger, put my feet up on my new desk, and popped some juicy fruit into my mouth. I chewed it assiduously and exactingly. It has to be chewed to exactly the right consistency for the maximum facilitation of cogitation.

I tried to think about Hojas. All I could think about was Hojas's sister. And what'd happened the night before.

Real smart, Kamus, I told myself. On some level, you must've known what the intimacy of the mindsharer might bring.

But it was hard to regret an experience that powerful. It had been perfect, and I was going to see her again, soon, and if we found a free moment we'd find some more perfection.

Think about Hojas. The electronics he'd brought into town. That was the key. Find out what they were. Maybe deduce from that knowledge the nature of his power.

The phonecub rang again. Gingerly, I reached for it. Maybe I'd forgotten to feed it . . . It suffered me to pick it up and Andalaya's voice came out of it. "Kamus—it occurred to me that those electronics Hojas brought into town might be the key. I thought if I could find out what they were we could perhaps deduce from that knowledge the nature of his power."

I grimaced. "You really ought to leave the detecting to the detectives. So you don't put us out of work."

"I thought the first thing we ought to do is find out where the stuff is now. I went to ask Hojas—I had a pretense all worked up—and he was gone! Sperb knows nothing about the electronics and says that Hojas has left Mariyad. I have no idea where he went or how to reach him. He doesn't have a phonecub. Doesn't trust them."

"Smart. Phonecub might pull off a coup, try to replace him with itself."

"Is that a joke?"

"Is a cripple a star sprinter?"

I knew what I had to do. Boy, would Captain Sark be glad to see ol' Kamus again . . .

Right.

"I can't do it," Captain Sark said.

"Sure you can. Here's the trick: Don't tell anyone but me." I smiled and spread my hands. "Simplicity itself."

"I have my orders—and my orders are not to give you diddly-squat."

"Then we're in business. I don't *want* diddly-squat. I want to know where they shipped the imported electronics to."

She looked at me like I was a bug on the wall, and she was trying to decide whether or not the bug merited the effort to get up, walk over to it, and squash it. "Kamus, I don't like to be high-pressured."

"You said you wanted to know what I found out. How can I find out anything if you plug up my means of finding out?"

She sighed. I had her there. "Close the goddamn door."

I closed the door to her office. She pressed a button on her desk and a little computer console rose from its flat surface, and asked her, "What can I do for you, Captain Sark?"

"You can give me a keyboard. I don't want to vocalize this. And after I deactivate you, forget it all."

"No problem, Captain Sark!" A keyboard rose up out of the top of the desk. She accessed the customs database and asked what destination Buckfinster's imported gear had been shipped to. She had to give the computer a tedious series of access codes. After a moment she looked up from the screen.

"This won't be much help. It went to a shipping company in Mariyad. Crosswell's Crosscountry Shipping."

"That helps some. Crosswell only ships to the South and West. When did it go out?"

"It left the airport for Crosswell's yesterday."

"Then I'd better get over to Crosswell's."

I turned to go. She said, "Hey, Kamus."

I turned back to her. "Yes?"

"You owe me."

"Right." I went out onto the concourse. It was almost noon and I was in a hurry. Had to get to Crosswell before the stuff left. Across the square I could see construction workers in nulgrav harnesses, moving through the air like worker bees as they used sealants on the reconstructed Unity tower. The sealants made a loud crackling noise as they refabricated the bonds between the metal molecules. I turned a corner, stepping into a dimly lit, deserted landing at the top of an escalator—and somebody kicked me hard in the pit of my stomach.

61

I folded up, coughing, and somebody else behind me snatched my sword away, threw it to one side, and kicked my knees out from under me. I fell as someone said, "Never mind the interrogation—just kill him." I rolled convulsively to one side and the harsh red beam of a blaster sizzled through the deck, just missing my head.

Wheezing for breath, I jumped to my feet and vaulted over the escalator rail as another blast seared the place I'd occupied a tenth of a second before. I fell heavily on the metal stairs, felt myself carried up . . . up toward the man with the blaster at the top of the escalator. Had time to see that it wasn't a man at all, it was a Tserg, a big salmon-colored alien with antennas where his eyes should be and a palp for a mouth, but otherwise looking human, wearing the same kind of suit as Draco had worn—and aiming the blaster at my head. I'd been fumbling for my pouch, and I flung a handful of stardust in his face.

We call it stardust. It's an incendiary dust that pops into a minifireworks display in the air when it's thrown. It formed a curtain of very temporary flame that made him stagger back, missing me again with the blaster but this time searing a hole through my collar and singeing the back of my head. I reached the landing, poised to jump at him as he got his footing and saw that he had a bead on me now—no time to chant a spell—

Draco was standing to one side, laughing—

I was going to die—

And then the Tserg seemed to lift up in the air, for no apparent reason. I saw the reason in the next instant. Captain Sark had come up behind him, had him under the armpits, and was pitching him against the wall easy as tossing a Styrofoam dummy. The Tserg slammed against the wall and dropped the blaster, but recovered and ran hissing at her like a Terran fullback about to make a tackle. She braced, smiled wickedly, and caught him with an uppercut, moving in a blur of speed, hitting him so hard I heard his exoskeleton cracking. He went spinning to one side, out cold.

I looked for Draco. He'd split.

Captain Sark was frowning at me, rubbing her bruised knuckles. "I was reading about detectives in the computer library. It's true what they said about them. Where a private eye goes, trouble follows."

"We *follow* trouble, too, so it's a kind of like we're running in circles. Thanks for being there. How'd you know?"

"I looked out my window, saw Draco and the Tserg follow you. I know the set of a Tserg's antennas when he's going to bump somebody off. I used to work on the planet Tserga. You okay?"

"Yeah." I picked up my sword. "So you noticed Draco, too. What you going to do about it?"

"Try to get a warrant out for him. Not easy. The Outfit's protected."

"Yeah. I'd like to find the little creep myself . . ." I rubbed my gut. "I'm gonna have some pretty colors just over my navel."

"You wanna escort out of the spaceport?"

"Naw, they're cooled for a while. You better see about that Tserg—looks like he's going to wake up. You need me to testify against him?"

"Uh-uh. I slapped up a camera—" She pointed at a disk with a tiny glass lens on it, affixed to the wall. "—when I got here." She pried the little evidence camera off the wall and stuck it in her pocket, then retrieved the blaster and pointed it at the Tserg. She glanced at me. "You going to tell me why they're trying to bump you off?"

"They know I'm on the case. They know I keep digging, I'll find the link between them and Hojas, and maybe some other stuff they don't want me to find. They don't want me to keep digging."

"Figured it was something like that. I might need you to sign something, sometime."

"Just say the word." I turned to go down the stairs behind the escalator.

She said, "Hey, Kamus."

I turned back to her. "I know. I owe you one."

"Not good enough. Now you owe me two."

Crosswell's was a low, broad warehouselike building of stone across from a row of taverns and sleazy bars, on the southwestern edge of town. A rutted dirt road led up to it on either side. Andalaya had called on my phonecub and proclaimed herself too restless to do anything but work on the case with me. She and I were across the street from Crosswell's looking out the window of the Lazy Cannibal Bar and Grill. On the old wooden tavern sign over our window was a faded painting of a cannibal eating a man alive. Most of the other patrons in the bar looked like they could've been closely related to the cannibal in the painting. A charming little place.

"How are you going to get them to tell you where the stuff is being shipped?" she asked. "This place is secretly run by the Kakush—they use it for drug running. They aren't likely to tell anyone anything, even if you offer a bribe."

I chewed a piece of gum meditatively, then said, "I think I've got a plan. Wait here."

I left the bar, crossed the street, and went into the office of Crosswell's Crosscountry Shipping. A man behind a wooden counter was filling a brass pipe with a noxious herb. He had a patch over one eye and someone had carved away the left half of his nose, once upon a time. He lit the pipe with a candleflame as I spoke. "I've come from Buckfinster," I said, snarling it, and generally looking displeased.

This is how it was supposed to go:

I tell him I've come from Buckfinster. I let him know Buckfinster and I—his assistant—are irate about a misunderstood shipping order. I then tell him that Buckfinster believes that whoever took his shipping order got the information wrong. We need to check that out, make sure you sent it to the right place. What destination do you have for shipping the goods—and when do they go? And by what route? Buckfinster wants to make sure of all of it. He's very careful about these things, if you know what I mean.

Whereupon the guy was supposed to blink stupidly and look at his shipping order scroll and say, "Says here it's going to—[the crucial information] at the hour of [further crucial information] and it goes by the route [the last bit of crucial information]. Does that tally with what you have, sir?"

Whereupon *I* say, "Oh, sorry, you've got it right after all. But while I'm here I may as well inspect the goods . . ."

That's how it was supposed to go.

What actually happened was this. "So you're from Buckfinster!" he snarled at me, showing greenish yellow teeth. "So bloody *what*?"

"Well, ah, Buckfinster's concerned—in fact, he's downright irate—as he thinks you may have the shipping order wrong, maybe sent the stuff to the wrong place—"

"If we've got it wrong then he gave it to us wrong! And if he don't like where it's going, that's tough, it's too late to change it, we've already sent it! The ship's on the way! And if the stuff were here I wouldn't change the destination because it's too damn much work to reload the stuff onto another ship! Especially on the say-so of a slimy little scum-worm like you! Now get outta here before I use your mouth to clean my private parts!"

And then, to add insult to insult, he blew smoke in my face. I put my hand on my sword. He drew his own sword and rang a bell that summoned three other big, ugly men, each bearing an enormous razor-sharp scimitar.

I smiled affably, tipped my hat, and said, "Wow, I'm late for a lunch date. Have a nice day." I backed away and stepped outside. Andalaya was just outside the door.

"I heard everything," she said, smirking. "Leave it to me."

Before I could stop her she went into the shipping office. I drew my sword, prepared to rush to her defense.

She spoke to the one-eyed guy at the counter for two minutes and came back. She smiled in a superior sort of way and took me by the arm. We strolled off down the street. She said, sweetly smug: "Buckfinster had the stuff shipped to Mount Veneris, in the Ja-Hadege Range. It went out four hours ago, on a ship called the *Soaking Rag* bound for Zipgaff, where the Black Desert meets the Inland Sea. And from Zipgaff it'll go cross-country by the western caravan trail to Mount Veneris—which is at the northwestern tip of the range."

I looked at her with awe. "Men *are* putty in your hands."

"No. Just you. I recognized the gent with the eyepatch. He was one of my customers. He might be Kakush—but he's scared of his wife. I told him I'd tell her about that little blond he liked to take bubble baths with if I didn't get the information. I've seen his wife—we keep track of those things in case we need them. She's bigger than him and twice as mean."

"Maybe he's married to Captain Sark."

"Who?"

"Forget it."

"What I can't understand is, why didn't Hojas use his supernatural powers to send the stuff through the air from here to the mountain he wants it to go to?"

"That," I said, "I can tell you. He's taking it to the land of the Darklord. Any magic—or significant energy manifestation—on his borders, the Darklord knows about. He would see it coming. Hojas is smarter than he looks."

"Don't insult my brother's looks. Well—we'd better find a ship to take us to Zipgaff, see if we can catch up with them on the Black Desert—"

"Hey, whoa. Look, you're a smart, capable woman but this is something I'd better do alone. It's dangerous out on the Black Desert."

"Don't be absurd."

"I mean it. I insist, Andalaya. You stay behind."

"You're firm on this, are you? You mean it?"

66

"Absolutely."

"Nothing would change your mind?"

"Nothing whatsoever."

"If you don't let me go, I'll never go to bed with you again."

"You'd better bring a coat. It's cold on the Black Desert at night."

Standing at the aft rail of the *Leaky Bladder,* a two-master whose sleekness belied its self-deprecating name, I looked out over the phosphorescent gleam of the ship's wake, luminous white against the deep purple of the sea, and wondered if I should contact the Darklord. I could tell him about the shipment we were tracing . . .

He might know already. He might be monitoring me—but I didn't think so. I hadn't felt his psychic touch, and I doubted he was keeping track of me as closely as he'd threatened. He was too preoccupied. Chances were, he didn't know about the shipment Hojas was sending to Mount Veneris.

But if I told him about the shipment, he'd probably destroy it—or try to capture it. Hojas would react, and the conflict would come to full bloom.

Between Hojas and the Darklord, I suspected, was the power to destroy Ja-Lur. Should they come into direct conflict, that power would be unleashed.

If I could just find the thing myself . . . identify the source of Hojas's power . . . I could, perhaps, find a way to nip the bloom of supernatural war in the bud.

But I didn't have much time. It took only a day and a half to sail to Zipgaff, under favorable conditions. The caravan had a considerable lead on me . . . I might not get there in time.

Maybe I should tell Jann-Togah. Maybe I shouldn't.

Andalaya interrupted my ruminations, joining me at the rail with a bottle of wine and two glasses. "We can't make the ship move any faster than it's going," she said.

"No," I agreed. "We can't." For in fact I'd already

called up the Elementals of the Airs to blow the ship faster on its way. Urged by these invisible zephyrs, whose sullen moaning haunted the ship, the *Leaky Bladder* surged through the waves with unnatural speed.

"So all we can do," she went on, pouring the wine, "is amuse ourselves till we get to Zipgaff." She passed me a glass of wine.

I drank it off and took her by the hand. "You're right again. You're always right. Let's stay in the cabin till we get to Zipgaff."

"You'll have to make trips to the galley to get more wine."

"And to the rail to get rid of some wine."

"You can use the window for that."

I kissed her and we went below.

The lugubrious moaning of the elementals had stopped. It was the cessation of this sound, and of the ship's rocking, that had awakened me.

Zipgaff was a depressing welter of huts built helter-skelter of driftwood and rushes and the round stones found at a seaside. I saw the crabbed little town through the porthole of our stateroom in the dull morning light, a day and a half after we'd gone below.

We were anchored at Zipgaff's tumbledown dock, not far from another ship: the *Soaking Rag*.

I was about to tell Andalaya to get dressed so we could disembark in search of breakfast—and, secondarily, clues—when I heard a chillingly familiar voice.

It was coming from the deck, just over my head.

It was Draco's voice.

VII

Heavy boots on the wooden deck over our heads. Lots of them. A squadron of them. And judging by his tone of voice, Draco was telling them what to do.

Chances were, he'd tell them to use those boots on my head.

We heard them coming down the ladder. "Now what?" I muttered, as we pulled our clothes on. "The porthole's too small for us . . ."

Not one for panicky responses, Andalaya shrugged, locked the door and blocked it with the bunk.

I turned my back to the door, twisted my fingers into the appropriate sign, pointed them at the bulkhead nearest the dock, and spoke Language. *"D'ammleshga fe'koh Te-Ir!"*

I felt the dark energies course through me, and out along my arm, then into the wall. The wooden planks blurred and shimmied as if viewed through hot air, then began to buckle. Outside the cabin door, men were shouting, banging on the door, at first in confusion and then in concert, throwing their shoulders into it. Andalaya heaved back from the other side of the bunk. The lock began to give.

Magically imbued with unnatural flexibility, the vertical planks in the bulkhead warped, and bent to the right and left, creaking, half of them one way and half the other, making an opening in the wall just big enough for us to squeeze through.

69

The ship was snugged up against the dock—and Draco had left no one there to watch for us. The bulkhead closed behind us a second before the door gave. I heard a clank and a splash and a multiple yell of juicy perturbation, and then we were fleeing down the dock to the village. The place smelled of fish; we dodged between heaps of fish guts and shells and clouds of flies, and ran between a series of ramshackle houses and huts.

When we paused to rest in a twisting alley, I asked Andalaya about the clank and splash I'd heard from behind us in the ship. "Oh, that. I poised our chamberpot over the door."

A girl after my own heart.

As luck would have it, I knew someone in Zipgaff. But unluckily, he had died a few months before.

He was at home nonetheless, and greeted us at the door. Andalaya gasped at the sight of him.

"Tix!" I said. "Good to uh, see you. You look, uh . . . well." I did such a poor job at the amenities because they were so patently false. Tix was a big man, with a long face and a mane of black hair. He was a former corsair who had built himself a cottage here for his retirement, and went on occasional forays as a mercenary. On the last foray, though, someone had done for him—I'd heard he was killed, and I could see the black-edged wound festering in his belly, for he wore only a loincloth and sandals. His hair had gone white and was falling out in patches—along with swatches of his scalp—and his flesh, gone green and blue, hung on his limbs like Spanish moss on a tree limb. One of his eyes was missing from its gore-caked socket. I thought I saw the movement of an insect within, but I wasn't sure. I didn't attempt a verification. His face hung like a coat on a peg. No breath moved his chest.

"My foggy eye," he rumbled, ever so slowly, "it lies to me. It tells me Kamus of Kadizhar has come. Can it be so?"

"It is, Tix. We need refuge."

"Then enter."

We entered with some reluctance: The place smelled

70

worse than the mindsharer's hut, though it was not a badly appointed little cottage. He barred the door behind us. We sat on a scarred wooden bench across from his bed; he sat on the edge of the bed, and I noticed bits of green flesh clinging to the bedclothes. My stomach lurched, but I managed a sour smile.

"Frankly, Tix, I came here thinking the place would be deserted. You were a feared man locally and I thought the natives would keep clear of it even after . . . well, I heard . . ."

He laughed, with a sound like a rusty saw on a chunk of hard wood. "They do keep clear of it—more than when I was alive. Oh yes, Kamus—what you heard was true. I was done for on the deck of the *Three-Legged Stallion*, run through with a cutlass. I lived till we made landfall on the island Berindi, where a local witchdoctor—who I have reason to believe was also of Darklander blood—said he could save me. He could not heal me truly—but he said that if I gave my consent, he could see to it I continued to walk in my flesh even after the wound had done its work. I was fevered and weak and not thinking. My mind was tormented by a morbid fear of punishment in the after-life—for this was what my mother predicted for me. I thought I could see the demons of Mother's Christian Hell waiting on the edge of my bed, sharpening their talons . . . hungry looks in their eyes . . . So I bid the witchdoctor to save me any way he could. He gave a chuckle—oh, I should have known from that chuckle—and he performed a ritual even as I died. I died, but my soul remained trapped in my body, though the body itself was dead, and in decay. I had the power of movement, I could indeed walk the world. I told myself it was better than nothing, it was life of a sort. But I could feel the Little Ones, chewing me up inside . . . And Kamus: I have a thirst that is never slaked." He reached one bony hand to a cabinet beside the bed and fetched out a pewter flask. He drank from the flask, and a moment later the amber liquor dripped out through the cracks between his ribs. He proferred the bottle to me and Andalaya. "Will you have a drink?"

"No thanks," we said, at the same instant.

"It is just as well. Bits of my mouth have fallen into the bottle—doubtless it has soured the taste. I wouldn't know. I can taste nothing."

"It's cruel, what the witchdoctor did to you," Andalaya said. There were tears in her eyes. I squeezed her hand.

"He did it with purpose," Tix said. "As a young man I was one of a drunken party of pirates who'd raided his island. We'd taken his daughter and sold her into slavery. Which is why, after we sold the girl, our ship disintegrated at sea, cursed by the witchdoctor, and most of the crew died. I only survived his curse by luck: Kamus came along, sailing out of Kadizhar, and found me drifting at sea, clinging to a timber."

I nodded. "I didn't know about the cursed ship."

"Shame kept me from telling you. I guessed it was a punishment for a misdeed. But I remained a corsair; oh, a raider of fat ships, after that, and not helpless islanders, but a corsair just the same. And then a mercenary—until the day I was run through. I did not know the island in my dying, but those many years later the witchdoctor knew *me*. What you see is his revenge—and I can't but wonder if the cutlass stroke that killed me was not guided by his hand in some way . . ." He took another futile drink and sighed with a sound like wind rustling drought-dry grass. Liquor ticked onto the floor from his belly. "He put me in a boat and pushed it out to sea, and the boat knew to take me here. And here I have lived—lived and died and lived and died—for nearly a year." He shook his head; a bit of ear-lobe fell off. "That is my longest speech since coming here. It is not easy to speak with the larynx of a dead man."

I told him something of our story, and he said he knew of the caravan we were following. "Being dead myself, I can hear the unbodied dead in their gossiping. I hear them now, whispering in the eaves of this cottage. And yesterday morn I heard them hailing a passing caravan, which carried a burden of unmade murders, so they said. It carried a machine that would make a sorcerer's killing easier, and would soon crowd the gate of the Deadlands with a great multitude. 'Murder marches to Mount Veneris,' they said. They were gleeful—wandering spirits become cynics, you know." He reached up to scratch his nose, and most of it fell into his lap. He sighed. "I wondered when that was going to go."

"Do you really believe a Hell-place of punishment waits for you after death?" Andalaya asked.

"Sometimes, when the fear is at its worst, I remember the superstition of my mother. The dead say they know of no such place—but they pretend to be otherworldly sophisticates, when in fact they are only those who have clung to our plane and wander here. There are many worlds beyond this one. I glimpsed them, as I died. But those gates are closed to me now."

"Tix's mother," I explained, "was educated by Christian missionaries from Earth. There were a number of them, a generation or so ago, until the Darklord declared that they were purveyors of destructive attitudes—frightening children with these stories—and had those who would not leave executed."

"I should certainly think so!" Andalaya said fervently. "A most enlightened decision!"

"Kamus," Tix said, looking at me imploringly with his one eye, "when I saw you on the doorstep I felt something that has been long lost to me: hope. Just a little flicker of it, but hope it was. Can you. . . ?"

"Perhaps," I said.

Andalaya raised a hand for silence; she cocked her head, listening. I heard it then myself: Draco's voice, and the sound of a group of men coming down the lane. And then the voice of a boy. "Aye, sir, I saw them run down here!"

They tramped up to the door of the cottage.

"Open up!" Draco yelled. "If Kamus is in there, his

ass is mine! Turn him over or we'll burn this dump down!"

"Leave this to me," Tix said softly.

We melted back into the shadows as he opened the door. He stepped out into clear view and said in his most lugubrious voice, *"Who troubles the sleep of the dead?"*

Men yelled and I heard booted feet in retreat. Draco was trying to hold his ground, stammering something, as Tix reached for him. *"You! Join me in my grave! It is so lonely! Come and embra-ay-ay-ce me-e-e-e!"*

Draco backed away, sputtering, "Uh—he's not there, that's for sure. Or if he is, he's dead!" He turned tail and ran after the others.

Tix turned to us, smiling a rotten smile and making the rusty saw sound. "I knew that zombie stuff would come in handy some time."

The hour was two strokes after sunset. The moons of Ja-Lur had risen and were in perfect alignment for the deed to be done. I lit the seven candles and arranged them in the shape of an arrow, pointing to the door and out to sea. Tix lay on the floor, in the diagram I had chalked there, trembling with anticipation and fear. Muttering: "If Hell awaits me—can it be worse than this? Or am I there already and suffering it as I speak, the delusion that I remain in the world of men being part of my punishment? The hope of an escape just another hell-torment . . . I feel the Little Ones: I believe they have burst through to my testicles . . ."

"Quiet, Tix," I said. "Don't distract me." I was taking a chance performing this ritual. It might attract the attention of the Darklord—or of Hojas. I wanted truck with neither one at the moment.

I focused, and stood on one foot, and cocked my head to the side, and curled the index finger of my left hand, and touched my eyeteeth together, and said, between them, something in the Language of Darklore so dark and sacred it cannot be repeated here. Andalaya, in fact, had on my suggestion put candle wax in her ears.

The dark energies curled up from the diagram, coiling around us like smoke from a fire, hot and toxic. My perceptions momentarily heightened, I saw the ghosts Tix had spoken of, seated in the rafters of the cottage, an uninvited audience, watching us and jeering and combing their fingers absentmindedly through their ectoplasm—a disgusting habit.

And then the cottage trembled. The door was flung open, and the spectre of an old woman stood there, the moons low in the sky showing through her—a sickle moon showing where her heart would be.

"Do not go," she rasped. "The punishment awaits you, son!"

"Mother!" Tix cried. "Leave me in peace!"

He squirmed on the diagram—and I was afraid he'd destroy the supernatural mechanism I'd constructed. So I spoke the final words and let the dark energies course through my arms and shiver through the air to Tix.

He went rigid, transfixed. I could feel a backwash now, a repercussion from the bonds that the old witchdoctor had set. And I saw the angry face of the witchdoctor, painted to resemble the fiercely striped head of a sea lizard, snarling at me from the darkness beyond the body of my friend.

"He's had punishment enough," I told the witchdoctor. "Back off—the Darklord stands with me!"

The witchdoctor's eyes narrowed. He looked and saw that I did indeed have a connection with the Darklord. He scowled—and then bowed to me. And faded away. But the ghost of Tix's mother was stepping into the room, her image changing from that of a small girl to a young woman pregnant with a child, to a middle-aged woman, to a sad-eyed old crone, all in a second. She was blurred with the aspects of her identity. "Tix—do not go! Hell awaits you!"

I held her back with a ripple of Darkness—and renewed my attack on the bonds that held Tix and felt them shatter.

Something that had clasped him slithered ethereally away, and then his corpse shivered from head to toe . . . and burst into a cloud of foul dust.

From the midst of the cloud emerged a smear of fluorescent blue, and I heard a music that was the melodic essence of gratitude and knew he was free.

His ghostly mother gave a cry of bitterness—until a fluorescent blue whirlwind encompassed her, swirled through her, and made her a part of itself. It carried her away, out into the night, and over the hooks of the horned moon.

We were trudging along the thin track that wound between the ebony dunes of the Black Desert, the stars glowering down at us, when Andalaya cleared her voice to ask something I was surprised it took so long to ask: "Kamus—can't you use magic and, uh—?"

"Carry us to our destination that way? No. I haven't that much power. I'm only a halfbreed Darklander, remember, and not the most educated in Darklore. And I'm feeling a bit enervated—helping Tix tuckered me out."

"That was a kind thing to do," she said. "It made me love you the more." Then she grimaced and smote her forehead. "I can't believe I said that. I sound like a limpid-eyed teenager. By the Darklord, if the girls at the bordello heard me they'd laugh me into respectability!"

I laughed and kissed her. "I rather like you as a limpid-eyed teenager."

"You're as sickening as I am. We're disgustingly gooey, Kamus. Let's do try to be more hard-bitten, all right? . . . But I'm glad you were kind to poor Tix."

"Maybe I was kind to him—but perhaps irresponsible for the rest of us. It cost us precious time . . ."

She was peering up at the sky. "And you have no power left? Not even enough power to control the mind of a pea-brained reptile?"

"What are you talking about? You want to ride there on sand lizards? Even if they trade off they're too small to—"

"No, you silly oaf. Look!" She pointed upward.

It took me a moment to see them. The pterodactyl-shaped places where the stars were blotted out. The silhouettes of kragor, two of them not far up. Big ones, too.

"No wonder I fell for you," I said. "I bet you could get a cab in New York during rush hour in the rain."

"What's New York?"

"Never mind. Let's see if I have enough power left . . ."

I muttered the words, and reached out with my mind. There was a shuddery cold-blooded *click*. I felt myself soaring on leather wings . . .

And then the kragor were flapping down beside us, with a creaking of leather and a snap of sickle-shaped beaks, their eyes glittering like dark gems. I carefully kept the hold on their minds—small minds, yes, but fierce ones—as we marched up to them. If I lost them, they'd attack us. That simple. These were feral kragor, undomesticated and bad-tempered. They'd sooner eat us than suffer us to touch them—let alone carry us on their backs.

I had ridden kragor before and climbed on mine first, tying myself on with my satchel strap, to show her how.

"I don't know about this," she said, staring at her own mount. "I think perhaps I was wrong. Maybe it was a bad idea. It looks hard to hold onto."

"Tie your satchel strap around its shoulders, and then wedge yourself under it," I said.

She approached the big flying reptile—and then stopped when it turned its head and glared at her, gnashing its beak.

"It's going to go for my eyes," she said. "That's what it'll go for first."

"I've got control of it," I said. "You'll have to trust me."

"It *sounded* like a good idea," she said. She sighed. "Very well." She put a hand up to protect her eyes and walked around behind the kragor. Its head turned to watch her every step. But it allowed her to clamber on and bind herself in place with the strap.

And then with a raucous cry it made a waddling running start, and lunged into the air, grabbing sky, gathering air

77

pressure under its twenty-five meter wingspan. My own mount followed and flapped laboriously upward. We rose steeply, and at first it was hard to hold on. I thought our improvised straps wouldn't work—and we'd fall together, Andalaya and I, and die a little distance from one another in the black dunes of the desert.

I struggled to maintain control and hold on, while fighting off vertigo. The longer I maintained control, the easier it would be.

And when we'd reached an elevation of a quarter kilometer the kragor leveled off and we found it easier to cling to our mounts. I could see Andalaya off to starboard, a ghostly-pale outline, her hair streaming behind her. I waved at her, without taking my arm out of the strap loop, and she waved back, though more tentatively.

It was cold up there. I hugged the back of my kragor for warmth. It smelled of vinegar and snakeskin. Its wings creaked and shooshed rhythmically, and my fatigue almost got the better of me. I nearly fell asleep. If I had, I'd have awakened in freefall—or in the kragor's talons. Sleep would mean losing control over the creatures. After which they would regard me in a different light . . .

Once, a few years back, I was chained near a man while he was disemboweled by a kragor. It had held him down with one foot while ripping open his belly with the claws on the other. Then it thrust its beak into his guts and began to feed on them. Took the guy a remarkably long while to die, through all this. I could still hear his screams . . .

The memory helped me stay awake.

Mount Veneris was not the highest mountain in the Ja-Hadege Range; but it was the final peak in the range to the Northwest, the sentinel that watched over the hills that separated the Black Desert from the Western Plains. It was an irregular cone, fissured and craggy, a great broken tooth of black stone. Its peak had been sheared off near the top in an ancient sorcerous battle, and the charred stump made a good landing place for the kragor.

ment she said, "You come up with anything

your plan before we came up to a mountain-
in the cold with all these thugs?"
ve one."
ou have a fine way of dealing with trouble,
leap headfirst into it."
my middle name, baby."
she asked seriously. "What's your last

ooks like they're almost through with that
s like trouble."
it looks like your middle name over there?
d."
you be so sarcastic when it's so cold?"
ey were constructing was composed of sev-
sections. All they were doing was bolting
together, connecting some wires, plugging
nto a fusion-charged battery unit. It didn't
onstruct. And the end result was something
e a cannon made out of giant vacuum tubes,
in its midst. The operator apparently sat *in*

wiveled it so it pointed to the South. To-
d, a target somewhere beyond the curve of
e Dark Spire. They were aiming it at the
elf, and the thousands of Darklord Loy-

rth, a bit of the sky became entangled with
ow it looked. When it got closer, we saw
eat blue star, twisting and dancing through
the cold winds before it so that the men on
p staggered and shielded their eyes. And
nking, depositing a man on the stone near
n.
, resplendent in a purple and gold parka,
and in hand. The men stepped back from

It was nearly dawn. I was shivering from cold and ex-
haustion, feeling my mental hold on the kragor slipping.
Once, my own mount had turned and snapped at me with
its beak.

I was glad to be free of them. My aching arms and legs
were glad of it, too. Andalaya moved stiffly into my em-
brace as, with a final effort, I sent the creatures hopping to
the edge of the mountaintop and soaring away.

"I'm glad that's over," I said. "I was beginning to
have strong urges to build nests and lay eggs."

Andalaya looked around. "So we're here ahead of
them. What now?"

What indeed. It was cold up there. There was a thin
deposit of snow on the knobs of rock around us, some of it
skirling in the pensive wind. The dark lid of the sky was
dented with the blue-white of morning, to the East. The
white-maned peaks of the Ja-Hadege Range trooping like
gray titans off toward the sea were austerely magnificent.

"Now—we need shelter and rest," I said. Looking
around I spotted a slash of darkness in the stone cap of the
mountain. We investigated and found a ravine. Descending into the ravine, we found a shallow cave beneath an
overhang. Andalaya spread out our bedrolls, while I used
the last of my strength to conjure combustion from a large
stone. Under the influence of a spell that tinkered with its
physics, the stone deteriorated into raw heat energy, very
slowly giving out the internal fires hidden in all matter. It
was an enormous lone coal, heating our stone refuge till
we were toasty and unable to keep sleep at bay any longer.

While the dim sun of Ja-Lur grudgingly escorted the
world into a new day, Andalaya and I slept deeply in each
other's arms.

I was awakened in late afternoon by a sound that didn't
belong to the mountaintop; a sound that had nothing to do
with the sough of wind or the hiss of snow on a rockface.

It was the sound of engines approaching.

VIII

The snow was marbled on the black stone around us; the wind bit our noses and ears.

Chewing condensed food bars and wrapped in long coats, Andalaya and I were on our bellies, side by side, peering down the cliffside at the vehicles moving up the steep mountain roads far below.

"They must've switched from pack animals to those vehicles somewhere outside of Zipgaff," I muttered.

From here they looked like toys, but they were massive yellow vehicles on massive wheels, jouncing from side to side on the rocky trail, spouting streams of blue smoke.

"Are those cars?" Andalaya asked.

"Of a sort."

"I saw some mechanical vehicles when I took the tour of the spaceport, but they were a lot smaller than those. Look at that smoke coming out of them! What are they burning?"

"I don't know. Fossil fuels, maybe. They're cheap and any world with much life on it has a supply of them. The Outfit probably set up a porta-refinery somewhere."

"But if everybody had a vehicle like that it'd poison the air!"

I nodded. "That very thing—and related mistakes—almost killed Earth a few centuries back. It's a bad habit.

And it's the sort of thing w[...] they take over here . . ."

"An industrialized worl[...] everywhere?"

"Right. And endless h[...] chises. Fast food places. [...] *delicious variety of anim[...]* chise: *Pork Parts*. And m[...] tion and planetary rapin[...] modernization I can app[...] Unity will bring, in care[...] sphere. But unlike the Un[...] technology—whatever loo[...] gard for the side effects [...]

"They're worse than t[...]

"Yeah. Probably. Th[...] Darklord."

"Look—the vehicles [...]

They had. Something [...] the biggest. Something [...] attracting the attention of[...]

We watched from the [...] miserably but afraid to [...] heat, as the copter arrive[...] spewing smoke and ra[...] noise. The men who [...] structed on the mountai[...] style and ease with the [...] thetic parkas may have [...] duction, too.

I looked for Hojas an[...] He was supervising, sm[...] resting in the crook of [...]

"They're sure to che[...] Andalaya whispered.

"Yeah. I know. I'm[...]

After a m[...] yet?"

"Uh-uh."

"What wa[...] top to shiver[...]

"Didn't h[...]

"Lovely. [...] Kamus. You [...]

"Trouble'[...]

"Really?" [...] name?"

"Smith. [...] thing. It look[...]

"You mea[...] How awkwa[...]

"How can [...]

The thing [...] eral different [...] those sections [...] the machine [...] take long to c[...] that looked lik[...] with a cockpi[...] the cannon.

Now they [...] ward, I guesse[...] the horizon: t[...] Darklord him[...] alists.

Off to the n[...] itself. That's [...] that it was a g[...] the air. It drov[...] the mountaine[...] then it was sh[...] the glass cann[...]

It was Hoja[...] globe-tipped w[...]

this apparition—all but Draco, who strode boldly up to him.

At this distance, their words were lost to me. I muttered Language, focusing the power on the stone at my feet. *"Bizz zebah De-evesdrah puhzz!"*

Their voices were carried magically to the stone, and Draco's voice emanated from it. ". . . it's ready for you, near as I can make out from those assembly diagrams. I hate that insert tab *A* into *B* stuff, I always get it wrong."

"Nice trick, the eavesdropping rock," Andalaya whispered.

"Could have better fidelity if it had some woofers and tweeters," I said.

"What's a woofer? And what's a tweeter?"

"Never mind."

One of the men stepped up to Hojas, a man in a mountain cloak whose face I saw for the first time. It was Buckfinster. ". . . No time to waste," Buckfinster said. "I've been in communication with Sartoris. The Darklord is closing in."

"Where is Sartoris now?" Hojas demanded. "He must triangulate in a timely fashion!"

"He's on his way," Buckfinster said soothingly.

"He should have been here by now! That was how I ordered it! Let no one forget who is in command here!"

"Hey, the guy'll show, man, just chill out, okay?" Draco said.

"It might not be wise to . . ." Buckfinster paused to look for a diplomatic way to put it. "To discuss the matter of command and, ah, hierarchy, when Sartoris arrives. He's accepted matters as they stand, of course, but he's a bit touchy on the subject—"

"He must understand absolutely and completely!" Hojas boomed in his most pompously ringing tone, "I am the destiny of this world! His lot will be governorship of the South—as agreed!"

"Sure, sure, right, a deal's a deal," Draco said.

Andalaya shook her head mournfully, murmuring, "Oh,

god, Hojas, you've got yourself in it up to your neck. You don't know what you're doing or who you're doing it with." She looked at me with round eyes. "Kamus—they'll kill him."

"Maybe not. Maybe he'll protect himself with his power," I said, not believing it.

I felt the approach of a powerful Darklander then. It was like the approach of a spider on a web—I felt the quiver of its movement on the web strands of Darkness. Suddenly the air over the mountaintop erupted as if from an invisible volcano. And from this fissure in nothingness came fire, sulfurous smoke, beams of red light . . . and Sartoris.

The workmen threw themselves to the ground at this display of magical potency, and even Draco and Buckfinster stepped back, uncertain of themselves.

Sartoris was twice the height of a tall man—he'd chosen to be tall enough to tower meaningfully over Hojas and Buckfinster and Draco, but not so tall as to make communication difficult. He was swathed in black, with only his oval face showing: a classic Darklander face, with its high cheekbones; dark, sardonic eyes; cruel lips.

"Greetings," he said, his voice supernaturally charismatic. "I am Sartoris, the rightful Darklord of Ja-Lur."

Hojas scowled. "Darklord only of those lands that I—"

Buckfinster interrupted hastily. "There's no time to attend to details. Jann-Togah must be aware of us by now. We must act quickly lest he interdict the operation of the amplifier with a renewed mandate against technology."

"I have already used my spirit slaves to protect our technology against any such mandate," Sartoris said. He glanced our way—I shrank back behind the rock but felt his gaze nonetheless.

Hojas waved his wand—and was transformed, to a giant three times the height of a man, so that he stood head and shoulders over Sartoris. "I too have protected our equipment. You need not have bothered."

Sartoris muttered Language and was suddenly four times the height of a man. Taller than Hojas.

Hojas raised his wand—

Buckfinster put his hand to his forehead, as if he had a migraine. "Gentlemen! This is no time for supernatural one-upmanship! Hojas—I humbly advise you to enter the glass cannon immediately."

This would mean reducing size. The idea obviously didn't appeal to the scowling Hojas. But he shrugged and shrank himself to man-size, then levitated, floating up and into the cockpit of the glass cannon.

Sartoris took his place at the cannon's side. Buckfinster puttered around the equipment, talking to a technician. "You're sure the amplification won't rupture the stasis field?" Buckfinster asked him. "There was another incident of the sort on Carcosa and they lost a continent to it."

"Massless singularity isn't hard to keep in its stasis field," the technician replied. "There's another variety of quantum singularity you're thinking of. This one's from Carcosa but it's got different energy configurations. Of course, my instruments do show a small leak—we could plug that with a—"

"No, no! The leak is the source of the reality instability! The small leak is just what we want—it's a full scale rupture that worries me."

"Not much chance of that right away—but the field could become unstable with all this energy emission that comes when he uses it . . ."

"So that's it," I murmured. I'd heard about Carcosa. A planet in the forty-third Galactic quadrant, notorious for irresponsible experiments with quantum singularities taken from an exploded black hole in a contiguous star system.

"What's it?" Andalaya whispered.

"The source of your brother's power. A quantum singularity—basically, it's a tiny black hole. You know what a black hole is?"

"The Great Out-House of Holovan is sometimes called a black hole."

"Not the same thing. A black hole is the result of the gravitational collapse of a massive sun. It's imploded on

85

itself, super-compressed, so gravitationally powerful it pulls light into itself—and anything else around it. Unless you have it in the proper containment field. A quantum singularity is a tiny fragment of a black hole. These things crush matter and energy up and crush the laws that control them at the same time—the laws of physics are warped around them, as a result, and so are the laws of time, space, and dimension. Reality itself can spontaneously shift around a singularity—and some people have claimed that this reality warp could be controlled by a properly trained mind using the telekinetic energies of the subconscious."

"Sounds like bullshit to me."

"It is. But it's the closest I can come to explaining how these things work. Your brother's got a black hole quantum singularity in a containment field, if I've got this thing sussed out right—and he's using the power of his mind to control the leak of reality-warping wild card energies from that field. Didn't you once tell me that he mastered the Four Mental Disciplines of Charlatanism?"

"Only three of them. He could never get trigonometry right."

"Evidently he got the control-of-secret-subconscious-energies part right. Anyway, the point is, his magic isn't magic as we know it—it's an exploitation of an aberration of the laws of physics."

"How do you know that isn't what real magic is? Do you *really* understand how the inner mechanisms of magic-as-we-know-it work?"

"Not really the inner mechanisms," I admitted. "Smart aleck female," I added, grumbling.

"But what's all this got to do with the glass cannon?"

"From what I've heard, it's some kind of amplifier—and projector, looks like—for Hojas's power."

Power, I thought, *they intend to use against the Darklord.*

I had to stop them. I had no doubt that this attack on the Darklord would escalate into full-blown war. And the petty, self-indulgent personalities here on the mountaintop would not be the ones to suffer. Or if they did, it wouldn't matter to me. The ones who'd suffer would be, as always, the innocents: the farmers, the shopkeepers, the artists and artisans, the fishermen—and their children. The people of Ja-Lur, crushed under the boot heel of war.

The hell with that.

I raised my cold-stiffened fingers and, softly, began to chant.

On the other side of the mountaintop, the cannon had taken on a violet glow. Taken it from the globe on Hojas's wand. The shimmer had oozed down the wand, which was plugged into the cannon like a stick shift in front of Hojas. The singularity's energies shone like foxfire, a light shifting from violet to white to violet again, intensifying in the heart of the crystalline tube, becoming a ball of incandescence; the glow increased and with it came a sound like a giant slowly inhaling, preparing to let go a hurricane . . .

Sartoris stood on the far side of the cannon, one hand raised, his eyes fixed on some distant point in the South— the Dark Spire probably—as he prepared to focus the cannon's fury, helping to aim it precisely at his enemy, the Darklord.

As all of this sank in I continued chanting, drawing what power I had up into myself. I'd need all I could lay my hands on. Even then it would only be enough if I applied it just right . . .

My plan was to open a rift into the Seventh Dimension, which I knew to be a sort of limbo that simply absorbed energy and flattened out its curves and peaks. Energy became neutralized there. If I could propel Hojas's singularity into the dimensional rift, it'd be disposed of safely.

If I simply interfered with it, cataclysm would result. But there'd be cataclysm if I didn't try.

The mountaintop was shaking, rumbling with the energies unleashed. The faces of Hojas and Sartoris were strained with concentration. A slow whirlpool of astral fogs gathered overhead, centered above the cannon. Its glow was becoming difficult to look at, like the blue-white heart of an acetylene torch's flame. Buckfinster and the others shrank back, behind the cannon, shielding their eyes.

The cannon was about to fire . . . I could feel it . . .

And then I felt I had connected. Someone in the Next World had picked up the phone.

I stepped out of the ravine and opened the gate to the Seventh Dimension.

The sky rang like a gong and the gong broke, shattered down the middle, as the rift opened in front of the cannon. I held it open with the energies coursing through my left arm while with my right I fired a beam of cutting energy at the wand, trying to knock it into the dimensional rift.

But I was too slow. I just didn't have the power or the skill to do it rapidly. Sartoris was there, suddenly, hovering over me, countering my energy bolt with one of his own, and the two fires contended—and mine lost. It went spinning awry.

Into the cannon. The glass of the cannon shattered and its inner fires roared upward, blasting Hojas one way and his wand another. The rift into the Seventh Dimension closed. And as for the wand containing the quantum singularity . . .

Sartoris and I both turned to look, as the wand's globe burst on the stone, its substance weakened by the errant energies of the cannon, and the containment field was exposed, for one millisecond: a cage of quivering nonspace. And then it too shattered, but like a soap bubble that splits into other bubbles it became three smaller fields that rocketed about the mountaintop like meteors invested with Brownian motion, ping-ponging off nothing at all, passing through stone as if it were fog and through men as if they were less than fog. Sartoris spun out an energy skein and tried to trap them, but they whipped away, as if purposefully evading him, and rocketed away from the mountaintop, screaming through the air like outgoing missiles, leaving a burning trail behind them.

The singularity had split up into three smaller singularities. Which vanished over the horizon, in three directions. Vanished into silence.

For a moment the only sound on the mountaintop was the sigh of the wind and the moan of a man whose middle had been neatly burned away when a singularity happened to pass through him. After a moment he finished dying, and then the only sound was . . . a thunderclap, as Sartoris clapped his hands together in fury. The mountain shivered with the repercussion.

"YOU!" he bellowed, livid with rage, pointing a finger at me.

"Yeah," I said, feeling a little sick. "It was me. Just doing my job. No extra charge. In fact, it was on the house. I could even buy you lunch on my expense account."

"I thought I sensed you nearby. I was in a hurry, didn't take the time to investigate. A mistake. And now a great opportunity is lost and someone has to pay. It will be you, Kamus. You will pay dearly."

"I just *offered* to pay," I pointed out. "Long as the place isn't too pricey. I know a cozy little café in the Thieves' Maze . . ."

I didn't feel as light-hearted as I was trying to sound. I was afraid of what the singularities might be doing, wherever they'd gone. I might've made things worse for all of us . . .

And what had happened to Hojas?

I turned and saw that he lay nearby, broken and bleeding. Andalaya was crouching beside him, holding his head in her lap. He didn't look good.

"I just . . . wanted to be someone else . . ." Hojas rasped. And then his eyes fixed on the greatness he'd aspired to. And saw nothing else.

Andalaya looked up from him, tears running down her

cheeks. "Damn you, Kamus! You killed him!" She pressed her face to his motionless breast.

"Andalaya—" I took a step toward her.

Bars of white-hot phosphorus stopped me.

A cage of blazing metal had formed around me, sizzling into being out of thin air. I felt myself enervated, my magics torn from me. Another cage formed around Andalaya, this one of cold steel, and lifted her weeping from the body of Hojas, into the air.

I turned to Sartoris, the builder of these cages, who remained hovering upright near me, glowering. "I could contract the bars of the cage," he said musingly, looking at me, rubbing his chin. "Slowly. Very slowly. The phosphorus would burn its way into you. Slowly. Your flesh would hiss and pop, Kamus. The notion is amusing. But not sufficiently amusing. I think I'd prefer to introduce flesh-eating imps into your bloodstream and see what they do to your brain, what they turn you into. That would be exquisitely painful and humiliating and could take months. Yes, there is merit in the idea. Or perhaps a wasting disease. Something to break down your immune system. I could let you get close to dying, then cure you, then infect you again, and so forth, for a century or two. Keep you cured for all of an hour. Just to give you time to think about it. Or I could cook your legs while keeping your upper parts alive so you could watch as I feast on your limbs—and feed your genitals to my hounds . . . Or maybe I'll crush your body slowly, over a period of days, between two compressing walls, and then just as you die extract your consciousness and inject it into another body and crush that one and do it again and again."

"Okay," I said, "I've irritated you. I understand that. The point is taken. Maybe I stepped out of line here."

He looked at me thoughtfully. "Or perhaps I could simply feed you broken glass. There's a certain simpleminded charm to that. But no, something more stylish. Flay the skin from you and then let a colony of fire roaches at you. They like to keep their victims alive so the maggots have something juicy to feed on when they hatch in your flesh."

"I mean, I blew your plans, you've had a rough day. But there's an inherent danger in overreacting. And I meant what I said about that free meal. Including dessert and capuccino." I knew this kind of talk wasn't going to get me anywhere. But it did more for my self-respect than wailing, 'Nooo-ooo pleee-ease don't!'

"I could open your skull, and extract little bits of it, a little at a time, at random, and just watch to see what happens. Even more stylish: extract your nervous system and brain from your body, but keep them alive and feeling, and make them into a living lampshade. With a five-hundred watt bulb."

Draco had walked up and was listening, grinning nastily. "All that stuff you got planned is too good for him. You want to really hurt him, hurt that bitch first." He nodded his head toward Andalaya.

The heat from the cage was making me look longingly at the snow, but I went cold inside at Draco's suggestion. "The girl has nothing to do with this, Sartoris. She only came to find her brother. She's suffered enough."

"If you care for her, she has not suffered enough. She matters to you, therefore you will see her die before you begin your eternity of suffering . . ." His eyes smoldered. The white-hot bars of the cage began to contract. To close in on me. "Perhaps a little disfigurement before I begin the other treatments . . ."

I hugged myself, hunching over, feeling the heat growing around me, my skin already beginning to hurt. Nothing to what I would feel in a moment. I had no magic left—but I had my potion pouch.

Surreptitiously, I reached into my pouch for the little rubber tube of Elf Stench. It contained an extract from the scent gland of Skunk Elves . . .

I squeezed the tube between the bars, shooting the mist into Sartoris's face. He shouted something inarticulate and staggered back, clutching at his eyes, cursing the awful smell. It was a smell like ten thousand locker rooms at half time combined with the reek of the Great Out-House of Holovan, with a few thousand dead-for-a-week Earth skunks thrown in for good measure. And maybe a half dozen road-killed possums. I gagged—but it had the result I'd wanted. Sartoris found it impossible to concentrate and the cages vanished from me and Andalaya. She fell a few meters to the stone beside her brother, landing on her feet. I ran to her, grabbed her hand and yelled, "Come on, we'll—"

She wrenched away from me and spat in my face. "Murderer!"

I stared at her. She couldn't see beyond the pain of losing her only blood relative. "Look, I—"

And then I heard a roar behind me. Turned to see Sartoris lurching toward me, blinking tears from his red eyes, gesturing in an arcane sign that, loosely translated, meant, *Death for Kamus*.

"I am going to give myself the pleasure of killing you NOW!" he grated.

A ball of fire appeared between his hands. It had my name on it. Literally. At least it was spelled right.

The fireball hurtled toward me—and I knew there was no dodging it. It would follow me, would seek out he who belonged to the name it bore, and it filled my vision, and . . .

And hissed away into a cloud of steam.

It dispersed, and I saw the Darklord, standing a little ways off, very casually, in the center of the mountaintop, one hand upraised.

Somewhere in the background, Draco and Buckfinster were legging it out of there in the copter, leaving a number of frightened workmen behind.

The Darklord wore an intricately inlaid suit of armor, both ceremonial and sorcerously potent; it was made of black metal flecked with gold, intaglioed with silver.

"Did you really think, Sartoris," the Darklord asked,

"that you could make such rude displays on my mountain-tops without attracting my attention?"

"Your mountaintops? You are not the rightful ruler of the South, Jann-Togah—as the will of the people will soon demonstrate."

"Liar! You have subverted their will with your own! You are subtle with bumpkins—match your own will to mine!"

Sartoris sneered and said something in an ancient tongue, something I didn't understand. Whatever it was, it ticked the Darklord off but good. He snarled and snapped off an energy bolt at Sartoris. But the would-be usurper had already raised a shimmering force field that deflected the black fire. Within his protective bell Sartoris floated upward—and then reached out telekinetically and sought to take both myself and Andalaya with him. I felt him wrenching at me—and then I felt the Darklord's power wash Sartoris's grip away, like the force of an inexorable tide. But in the course of this psychic arm wrestling I was thrown to the ground, and when I got unsteadily to my feet I saw Andalaya and Sartoris together in the belly of a cyclone, a shimmying column of black rising into the heavens. Too weak to do anything else, I watched help-lessly as they receded into the sky.

"Dammit, Jann-Togah, *do* something!" I shouted.

He was already chanting, making the signs.

He was a moment too late. A thunderbolt of angry red flashed down from Sartoris and struck the Darklord, con-suming him in fire, raging around him like a miniature nuclear explosion. After a few moments he bellowed Lan-guage, and it huffed out, extinguished. The Darklord stepped out of the smoking socket unscathed.

But by then Andalaya and Sartoris were gone.

IX

"I managed to lay a spell of protection on her," Jann-Togah said, "but I could not wrest her from his grip without destroying them both. He cannot hurt her. But he can carry her away."

I looked at him with some surprise. We were in a levitation bubble, drifting up over the mountain. Leaving the Outfit's workmen to descend as they might. He'd ignored my suggestion that he help them get down.

My surprise had come when he admitted he could have destroyed Sartoris—and didn't. In order to save a mortal.

"You getting morality in your old age?" I asked him.

He snorted. "I have been musing on the same puzzlement. Sometimes, when one is dealing in the Higher Energies, there is a sort of unexpected energy feedback, a resonation from some . . . well, from a place of the Widest Perspective. And one is moved to an apparently pointless mercy. But nothing from that higher place is really pointless."

I demurred. "You felt bad for her. You had an impulse to pity. You don't have to trick it up with all that—"

The look on his face shut me up. It was contempt.

Okay, so there are a few things I don't necessarily understand. He didn't have to look at me like *that*.

I was razzing him just to take my mind off the ache in my gut. Something had been wrenched from me when Sartoris snatched Andalaya. She was safe from physical harm for the moment . . . But she was still Sartoris's prisoner. And he'd use her, somehow. Some way.

Maybe it was my fault. Maybe if I'd stayed out of it. Maybe if I'd brought the Darklord in earlier, instead of trying to take care of it myself. Maybe if I hadn't acted like I knew what I was doing . . .

There hadn't been any time for those considerations, I told myself. I'd done what I had to.

But it hurt. It hurt.

Hurting inside, I drifted in a translucent black bubble off to the Southwest.

"You're going *where?* And *when?* And you're leaving me . . . *here?*"

"Are you hard of hearing, Kamus?"

We were in the Zank Swamp, at the headwaters to the Ja-Kanak River. It was close to evening. The gnarled, moss-laden trees seemed to stretch their out-reaching limbs in hungry anticipation, in the shifting mists rising from shadowy pools. It was warm and humid and insect-restless here. And I was shortly to be abandoned here.

And I didn't like it here.

Jann-Togah, the Darklord, went on, "I'm returning to the Spire. I must be near the totems of my power, in order to direct the campaign against Sartoris. If I'm gone any longer, he will use my absence against me, and on my return I'll find I'm no longer the Spire's tenant. I can take you no farther, nor can I waste further power on you. Your own powers, meager as they are, will return. And I will send two . . . individuals. To help you."

"Yeah? Who?"

"They are called Slim Shim and Slam Sham. They'll catch up with you, soon enough. In the meantime, you now work for me. Exclusively. Seek out the singularities and contain them, in this. Bring it close enough, and it will attract and trap them." He handed me a wand rather like Hojas's—but with a jet-black globe on the end.

"This good for anything else?" I asked him hopefully, looking at the wand. "Magic?"

"It is good for something else. It telescopes out to make a tent pole."

"Great. Fine. I'm all taken care of, then. If I had a Boy Scout knife I could scale fish."

"Why would you want to climb a fish?"

"Never mind. Look, I don't want to locate the singularities. Send some other toady to do that. I want to find Andalaya."

"She is in a fortress surrounded by a vast army and guarded by the most malevolent magics available. You cannot rescue her without me. If you find the singularities, I will have the power to overcome Sartoris—without a great war. That is the only way."

I hate it when I lose an argument. Especially when it means I spend the night in the Zank Swamp.

But I had a last shot at getting out of it. "You could protect me with a spell or use magic to locate the singularities and then transport me there—"

"No. The singularities, because of their nature, cannot be detected with magic. You will have to find them the hard way. And I can't spare the energy for a protective spell. I have faith in you. You can do a little thing like staying alive. It's the big things you fumble."

I winced. He meant my *faux pas* at the mountaintop. "Nobody's perfect."

"Some aren't even near it. Good luck. Bear northwest from here."

And then he stepped into himself, folded up, and became part of what wasn't there.

I was alone in the Zank. The feverish, hungry, humid, boggy Zank Swamp, which only really wakes up at night.

It was getting darker and darker.

I sighed, and, hefting the wand, I headed northwest. I took two steps and sank into something's mouth.

A disgusting creature. It's called a Lovelace. Some zoologist from Earth, a fan of antique pornography, named it after a woman who appeared in an old movie called *Deep Throat*. It's a shame, really. I've seen pictures of her. *Her* I could sink into, with no complaints.

The Lovelace, though, is essentially a giant slug that buries itself vertically in the ground, head upward, then opens its mouth wide and allows leaves and dust and the like to coat it for camouflage. So you stepped in its mouth, thinking it was only a slight depression in the ground, and it closed its jaws and began to suck . . .

I was up to my waist, before I realized what was going down, as it were.

My sword was clamped out of my reach. I was trapped.

Trapped again. That was beginning to be some kind of motif in my life. Crushed in Hojas's giant fingers. Strangled by the idiot-faced snakes of the Ziggurat of Zoln. Caged by Sartoris. Chewed and swallowed in the jaws of a Lovelace.

Trapped by responsibility; trapped by guilt.

The thing had nosed its head up above the ground in its eagerness to gulp me down. My lower half was going numb as it cut off my circulation and crushed my nerves. It shook me like a terrier shakes a rat, and I sank a few inches farther. Feeling the peristalsis of its throat working against my thighs and hips and groin. Dragging me down. Feeling below my feet a yawning void. There's emptiness at the heart of suction.

Pain lanced through my bones as I struggled, my pelvis threatening to crack. I reached into myself for supernatural energy, but it was too soon after the draining Sartoris had put me through—there was only enough magic in me to light a birthday candle. And I wouldn't see another one of those unless I could fan it into something more substantial. Maybe a small, precise spell . . .

I was in up to my armpits.

Make it fast, Kamus.

I remembered a small spell from my sorcerer's apprentice days, one that was used in the search for knowledge.

Any creature could be sorcerously made to take up human speech and explain itself . . .

Trouble was, I couldn't take a breath. The thing was compressing my diaphragm. Black spots swam before my eyes. I could feel its stomach acids nipping at my toes.

Straining with all my might, I managed to squeak, *"Gih meta Loh-dhnn!"*

The Lovelace stiffened and shuddered . . . and groaned deep within itself. Then it oozed upward, rearing out of its hole in the ground, and it spat me out with an inverted slurp.

I hit the ground on my right shoulder, and it hurt like a son of a bitch. I rolled and sat up, scrabbling away from the Lovelace, as it began its declamation. It cleared its throat and—towering ten feet over me, swaying like a dolphin dancing out of the water on its tail fins, slick and gray in the twilight—it spoke with a supernatural larynx: "I am the Common Lovelace, *Gastropodus Ja-Lurius Humongous,* typically ranging between one and four meters long and weighing up to one thousand pounds. My ventral surface is modified into a large, flattened foot which, along with other body parts, can be withdrawn into my burrow; the burrow is a replacement for the one-piece shell, or univalve, typical of many other gastropods—"

I was moving away to the northwest, clutching the singularity wand Jann-Togah had given me in one hand, with the other using a stick to probe the ground for other unexpected denizens of the swamp. The shadows thickened around me. In the distance, I heard the Lovelace reciting, in a voice like an oboe made articulate, ". . . I am believed to be related to the giant marine gastropod the 'Marilyn Chambers,' and am perhaps, as a swamp dweller, an intermediate form between the oceanic slug and the true land slug—"

I wondered how long it would have to keep it up.

Morning found me aching in the crotch of a tree.
I'd tried to pad it with moss. Didn't work very well.

My own limbs ached, creaking in silent accord with the tree's creaking, as I descended the slippery tree limbs and dropped to the soft turf. I looked down at my feet, half expecting them to sink into some enormous wet mouth or quicksand. But the ground was stable.

I looked around. The swamp had put on its finest for the dawn; its trees were stylish blue ideograms inked on the silver scroll of the fog. The light glimmered from ponds and sumps.

The night before, I'd struggled from one mound of solid ground to another, till finally giving up and using the moonlight to find a sleeping spot. I hadn't slept well, especially after something sinuous had slithered over me in the night. I'd remained very still, and it had gone away, but it left a residue of fear behind in me.

Now deeper fear flared up in me, as I thought again of Andalaya in Sartoris's hands. Could the Darklord's spell of protection around her really stand up to Sartoris's repeated mystical onslaughts? It seemed unlikely.

Maybe, I told myself, Sartoris is busy with his revolution. He won't take the time and energy to crack the protective spell on Andalaya.

I clung to that idea.

I trudged to the northwest, in a general sort of way, zigzagging from one root-clutched mound of damp, mossy ground to another, chewing the last of my food bars, wondering which of the local flora and fauna were safe to eat. I didn't know this part of Ja-Lur well. Though it seemed to me I'd heard something about a tribe of aborigines here. A surly bunch called . . . what, exactly? The Tribe of the Something Arrow. Red Arrow? Yellow Arrow?

Swiissss-shuck.

"Ah. The Tribe of the *Blue* Arrow," I said, looking at the blue arrow quivering in the tree trunk in front of me.

And then I ducked.

Another arrow pinned my slouch hat to the trunk. Imported hats suitable for Bogart in *The Maltese Falcon* are hard to come by on Ja-Lur. I risked my ass retrieving the hat, then crawled off into the shrubbery.

But they were all around me, jet-skiing around on the ponds, circling me like Indians around settlers. "I'm just passing through!" I yelled. "No plans to settle down!"

Mistake. The voice helped them locate me and another arrow nearly pierced both my ears at once. I'm not opposed to pierced ears in men but I'd prefer it done front to back.

As it was, the arrow grazed the back of my neck. Startled, I lurched forward, fell through the bush, and found myself lying facedown on the mud of the pond bank.

I hadn't drawn my sword. I wanted to look like I was no threat. I couldn't sword-fight a whole tribe of thugs armed with bows and arrows.

They stood around me, in the water, gaping at me. I gaped back at them.

They didn't have any legs. Their lower parts were melded into oblongs of flesh, shaped roughly like little boats but somehow very sleek and mechanical-looking. Resembling the jet-ski watercycles people on Earth use to destroy the peace of mountain lakes. Human skin covering the framework; an induction tube at the front end, a jet tube at the rear. Organic jet-engine boats. Seamlessly melded with human upper halves. I didn't know how they mated and I didn't care.

The black globe on the wand in my hand was tugging toward them . . .

So that was it. One of the quantum singularities had come to rest nearby. I was seeing a change it had wrought in the local reality . . .

And I remembered something Jann-Togah had said. *"The singularities will not alter reality entirely at random. Some of what takes place will be relevant . . ."*

The Outfit's mental influence had shaped these abominations. I'd seen their like in visits to the smoggy Outfit-dominated sections of Earth, in the truly mechanical mode. Watercycles, jet-skis, snowmobiles, three-wheelers, dirt-bikes, off-road vehicles. Machines that eat up the natural world, bit by bit. Here was a foreshadowing of what could happen to Ja-Lur . . .

They carried blue bows and blue arrows; their upper bodies were painted in red and blue stripes. The jet-ski part of each man sported a blue racing stripe. Their faces were fevered; their eyes glazed. Every so often one of them belched a little blue cloud of carbon monoxide smoke.

From what I'd heard, they'd once been perfectly ordinary aborigines, backward and surly but quite decent as savages go. Now they were a tasteless joke on humanity.

"Fellows," I said, smiling. "I was just stopping by to visit your chief. Bring a word of greeting from the Darklord."

One of them unwound a long strand of something from his shoulder. A moment later I realized it wasn't just a rope. It was a whip.

It cracked and encircled my neck, jerked me off my feet, and pulled me into the pond.

The water was warm. That's the best thing I can say for the experience.

I was dragged through the water behind a jet-ski man, the others laughing and hooting and racing beside me. I struggled to keep my face out of the water, but I was whirling like a lure on a fishing line, clawing at the whip, hearing the roar of the biological engines part of the time, part of the time only the muted sounds you get underwater. Slimy things wriggled past me; some of them had a rest stop in my underwear.

I was trying to draw my sword but it was hard without dropping the singularity wand. I was thinking: *Choked again. Trapped again.*

Enough was enough.

I clamped the wand in my teeth, dragged my sword free, and slashed the whip. The line parted and slackened on my neck. For a moment I spun in the bog, then I began to tread water—till I found I was standing in only three feet of it. I stood up, brandishing my sword, saw arrows winging at me, and used the sword to deflect two of them before they stopped coming.

They stopped because a gravelly, authoritative voice had shouted, "Stop!" Evidently, the boss of the Blue Arrows.

I looked around. The Blue Arrowmen rocked casually in the water like malevolent duck decoys, in a tight circle around me. We were in a sort of inlet, a little bay in a three-acre swamp island. On the gray mud of the bank, gray-brown huts ringed the inlet, made of reed and fronds and branches and mud, shaped in the cargo-cultist manner like ships and cars and planes. Things they'd never seen . . . There were pools of gasoline here and there, on the beach. The gasoline smell was almost overpowering.

The tribe's women and children were huddled back behind the huts. They were on wheels.

I didn't look too closely to see how that worked. No thanks.

I was staring at the Boss.

The lower parts of the jet-ski men were flesh-colored, though there was a certain hard metallic look to them in the sun; the flesh on the boss was going the color of blue s¢eel. Tan fleshtones shifting through a bruise spectrum to gunmetal. He was a ten-meter-high pyramid of metal and flesh, a sort of camouflage-pattern of the two colors and the in-betweens, a human head on top. To be precise, the pyramid shape started only after about the first few meters of him. The pyramid rested on a big, box-shaped base. The head was physically ordinary, like a middle-aged version of the brutish young faces that surrounded me—but the expression was as hard-edged and metallic as his body. On a thong around his neck was a chunk of raw crystal, and within it shone the warping, glowing taffy-pull non-shape of the quantum singularity, trapped within the field that kept it from sucking everything around it into a gravitational black hole. So this was where one of the quantum singularities had landed; it had inexplicably ensconced itself in a chunk of quartz. But where were the other two?

They might be anywhere. Doing anything to anyone.

I felt the wand clamped in my teeth tugging toward the singularity. I took it out—slowly—and held it in my left hand; my sword was at ready in my right.

The wand pointed toward the singularity like a dousing rod.

"You are a sorcerer?" the Boss asked. His voice had a metallic edge.

"Of sorts," I replied.

"A wet and bedraggled sort."

"At least I can move around," I said.

A certain recklessness in my choice of remarks can be attributed, maybe, to a struggle I was having trying to revive my sense of self-worth. I'd lost Andalaya; in my blundering I'd killed her brother. Now I'd let a bunch of warped primitives tow me by the neck through a bog. My self-worth was run over with a truck. Was bruised, bleeding, broken-boned, breathing shallowly, and there wasn't much of a pulse.

"I have no need to move around," the Boss said equably. "Things come to me. Observe."

One of the men stiffened and then turned, jetted up onto the bank. Glutinous wheels of bone emerged from slits on the underside of his chassis and he rode them up to the boss. A gap dilated in the front of the boss's big squat body, where none had been before. The man, glaze-eyed, rode into the gap. It closed, and there was a crunching sound.

"Now he is part of me, and I will grow," the Boss said. "And you will become part of me. And we will grow together. Perhaps I will have your sorcery when I take you in. I believe myself to be immune from sorcery— but perhaps I can wield it. Who knows? I know this: that you are conscious, *entirely* conscious, unlike these others, and you will be a choice sacrifice. You will be an exquisite delicacy."

I shook my head in amazement. Where had he learned to talk like this? Another effect of the singularity. I was scared to go near this great lump of rapacity. But I had to.

"You don't control me," I said, "like these others."

"I don't control you," he conceded. "But the second part of your statement is your doom. I control these others."

And then strong arms seized me, and began to drag me toward the gap dilating once more in the base of the Boss. Their god. They dragged me out of the water and up the mud beach, to a maw of metal and flesh. I saw a kibble of crushed bone and flesh in the raggedly shaped mouth. The warrior who'd gone before.

"You should close your mouth when chewing," I said, as they brought me closer. "But maybe you've never heard of Miss Manners."

"Good!" he said. And now the voice was rumbling out of the wet, blue-edged gap, echoing between the dripping membranes, carrying a stomach-twisting stench of carrion and motor oil out to me. "Good, laugh to the end! Hysteria adds a delicious aftertaste!"

I hoped I had this figured right. I was near that gaping two-meter-high mouth . . .

Looking down his throat.

I raised the wand and pointed it at the crystal on the thong. The crystal jumped on the thong, trying to reach the wand, yearning toward it. It quivered, there was a second of struggle—and then I felt a hideous quivering in the wand as the singularity was sucked into its black globe. The crystal fell back empty.

The men of the Blue Arrow Tribe cried out, and drew back from me. The Boss's hold on them was gone, at least for now—and they were in awe of the softly glowing black orb on the wand.

"Bring him to me!" The Boss bellowed. "Bring me the wand and feed me the man!"

"I control the power now!" It was a lie because the black globe sealed the power of the singularity away inside itself. It could wreak no more changes on the fabric of reality.

But I held the wand up for all to see. "I am now your God! Take me to the edge of the swamp, and I will quest to return your humanity to you!"

"Why would we want to be as we were before?" One of the halfmen asked me. He was the biggest of them, scarred and sullen. "We are more powerful now, and more mobile!"

"Have you got a dick?" I asked him.

He blinked at me. "Well. No."

"I rest my case," I said.

"You have a point," he said musingly, looking down at himself, then glancing at the females huddling in the huts. "Okay—I will take you where you wish to go."

There were mutters of dissent, and there was howling, quivering fury from the Boss. He shook like jelly on a plate in his anger. But they let me go, defying the habit of obedience. Probably, deep down inside, they'd always resented the Boss despite his absolute control of them.

I climbed onto the warrior's back, and he trundled to a pool of gasoline. He bent and drank from it. I had to hold my breath to keep from getting a face full of fumes. He straightened, smiling, and said, "Ahhhh! Very refreshing. It could use a little lead, though." Then we rolled to the water, and jetted across it and into the labyrinth of the Zank.

It was nearly sunset when we reached the northwest edge of the swamp. It ended at a field of dun grass that rose to become a hillside. "This is as far as I can go. I need to go back and refuel," my mount told me.

"Right." I climbed off him with a sigh of relief. I was fed up with riding him anyway. My ass was blistered and my legs and arms ached from clinging to him. Also, when he broke wind—or maybe it was backfired—I got sick from the monoxide fumes.

"Any instructions to us, now, since you're our new spiritual leader?" he asked me, in wide-eyed seriousness.

"Uhhh . . ." I hesitated. Maybe this was an opportunity to save the lives of other travelers. "No more preying on people who pass through. In fact, kill your boss when you get back."

"If I can kill him, I will. But we'll still want to kill other things. We *like* killing things."

"Well, just kill small animals."

He looked disappointed. "How small?"

"Ohhh, like . . . no bigger than this." I indicated a waist high spot.

"Yeah?" He perked up and asked eagerly, "So I can kill human children and babies?"

"Nuuuuuhhhhh *no*. Uh-uh. Wrong. Nothing human at all. No intelligent aliens either."

He frowned. "I think I'll change my religion."

He turned and skiied off into the swamp.

I turned my back on the Zank and climbed the hill. At the top I paused, and let the wand tug me toward the next singularity. To the West. I went a few steps—and then threw myself down in the grass.

A helicopter was coming toward me, throwing its insectlike shadow against the sunset light on the hillside.

X

I flattened in the grass, hoping they wouldn't see me.

It had to be Buckfinster and Draco. And Draco, at least, wanted me dead.

The copter buzzed by not more than a hundred meters up, not quite overhead. The grass was waist high, and with luck I'd seen them before they'd seen me.

I had. The copter continued on, ignoring me. It headed west. The same way I was going.

Could be they were outfitted with a technological version of the wand Jann-Togah had given me. Could be they'd get to the next singularity ahead of me. Yeah, could be. Seeing I was on foot and they had a goddamn *helicopter*.

Thanks for all the help, Darklord.

As the copter vanished over the western horizon, I got to my feet and trudged resignedly on. Ahead lay an unbroken sea of straw-colored grass and gently rolling hills. I took a stick of juicy fruit gum from my pouch and unwrapped it, popped it in my mouth, and put the wrapper in my pocket. I don't believe in littering. I chewed the gum, in preparation for some serious thinking.

I was thinking about that copter and what it portended: that Draco and Buckfinster were still part of the equation.

I shook my head in wonder at Buckfinster's stupendous obtusity. He put on sophisticated airs, but he'd never been far off-world. Two other nearby star systems. Big deal. He had no idea what he was in for, dealing with the Outfit. He couldn't have stolen the quantum singularity himself. It would have been watched the way a moneylender watches interest rates. It needed expert thieves. Maybe Draco. But Draco would have been suspect, if he'd been anywhere on Carcosa—so he'd have picked some greedy tourist, Buckfinster maybe, to smuggle the thing out for him.

Only, Buckfinster was just smart enough to check out the goods. And smart enough to know their potential. And just multiworldly enough to know that the Outfit was looking for raw new worlds to exploit—and probably had its eye on Ja-Lur. For at least a century the galaxy's big money had been frustrated by Ja-Lur, which abounded in kerium and oil and Thorazine crystals and other invaluable resources—the access to which had been proscribed by the Darklord. To top off the sundae, Ja-Lur was an Earth-type biological habitat—there weren't many of those left unexploited. It was a rough gem begging to be chiseled down into hot jewelry.

So Buckfinster, instead of holding onto the singularity for them until the time came, found a way to rupture the field. Dangerous tinkering. He was lucky to be alive. And found Hojas to take command of the singularity. And explained to the Outfit how Hojas and the singularity and Sartoris could be used to topple the Darklord. Technology didn't much work against the Darklord's magic. But a force that twisted reality to fit the whims of the mind could . . .

Maybe it didn't happen that way. Maybe the Outfit had had Ja-Lur in mind all along when they ripped off the singularity. And Buckfinster just happened to fill the right bills.

Yeah, that sounded more natural. And now Buckfinster saw himself as the necessary middleman who would be lazy in luxury once the Outfit took over. Had set himself a big, fat, swollen, belly-busting fee. And he was willing to barter the peace of a world for it.

The last glimmers of friendship I felt for Buckfinster died out. Ashes.

He was in for a surprise. Once they decided they didn't need him any more . . .

He was just a tool, like the Black Hole of Carcosa, used to pry up the Outfit's biggest obstacle to opening up Ja-Lur to organized crime and the ravages of overdevelopment. The Darklord. I'd done my homework on the Outfit. The Outfit's style was puppeteering. They'd move in and control the local government through graft, blackmail, death threats—and death that wasn't a threat. Chances were they figured they could use Sartoris as a puppet to keep the Unity at bay.

I had to chuckle at that one. They underestimated Sartoris. Ironically, they underestimated him the way Buckfinster underestimated *them*.

I knew that much, simply from looking into Sartoris's eyes. His Darklander blood had spoken to mine. He was going to hang onto every shred, every microcentimeter, every erg of his power; he was going to hang on like a vise-viper's lockjaw death grip. He was playing a waiting game with them. Let them think they could use him.

After they helped him topple the Darklord, he'd clamp the lid on the planet. He'd kick the Unity personnel off the planet and close their spaceports. He'd institute a blanket antitechnology spell, a mystical mandate that would mean that spaceships who tried to land would never make it—they'd enter the atmosphere and simply stop working and crash. The planet would be off limits, the new technologies on Ja-Lur would wither on the vine, and a new Dark Ages would roll over us all like a thousand-year fog . . .

Isolation was the Darklander way. Territory was the Darklander cloak of power. When in doubt, close in, shut down, and control. That was the Darklander psychology, and Sartoris was pure Darklander. Perhaps purer, as he indeed claimed, than Jann-Togah. But inbreeding wasn't likely to be what was best for the sorcerous people of the South.

Still, what was Dark Ages for the rest of us would be an age of comfort and pleasure for Sartoris and his followers. They take to shadows like night-adders and silver-owls, like blind fish in subterranean water; where there is superstition and uncertainty the Darklander thrives and allows his imagination to be fed, to be cultivated like mushrooms in a cavern. For the Darklander superstition easily becomes reality and reality becomes uncertainty and uncertainty breeds superstition as a sump breeds mosquitoes and the cycle goes on.

I remembered a warm, humid, brooding night, years ago, when I'd wandered in the South, in the Darklands, a fresh young man back from my first lengthy sabbatical on Earth. Aching after years on Earth to investigate my Darklander heritage. Get in touch with my roots, as the Earthmen say. I wandered on the edges of the dying city Treflegar, with Tix at my side. The young, living Tix, doing some landlubbing R&R. Tix was playing the man of the world, showing me the fleshpots of Treflegar, though in fact he was an outsider in this Darklander town, more profoundly than he knew. Though I had never been here before, it was I who belonged.

"The dying city of Treflegar," people said. How long had they been saying that? Forever, so far as I could discover. For hundreds of years. Its cachet, its mystique, was to die and die and die and never die.

Tix and I, that fulsome night, were strolling through the Grinn Quarter. "What you got to understand about whores," Tix was saying, "is that they're like beehives." There are beehives on Ja-Lur, brought a century before by Earth settlers, who'd simply interbred with the elder races of the Northern Kingdoms.

"Whores are like beehives?" I asked, baffled.

"Yep. If you approach them carefully and put out enough golden smoke and use them with caution, you get some sweet, sweet honey. You blunder into it and trust them too much, you'll make a misstep and you'll get stung. Sometimes stung to death. Your friends find you in an alley with a knife in your back and your purse gone.''

"Or in an infectious diseases ward with your dick rotting off. No thanks.''

"What's a dick?''

"It's old Earth slang for penis.''

"That's why I ask—it sounded that way, but seems to me you once told me it meant *detective*. You said you wanted to be a private dick. Did you mean you wanted to be celibate?''

"No, no, it's a homonym—''

"Hey, I'm not gay, man, just don't try any—''

"No, dammit, a homonym is a word that sounds—oh, never mind.''

"Come on, let's visit the whorehouse on Crotchfester Court. I'm telling you, it's all in how you use a whore—you got to understand the way they do business. They're like a beehive—''

"I don't think I've got enough pollen on me anyway. Or enough smoke either.'' We paused at a crumbling ruin, that made a melancholy occupation of a vacant lot, to watch a group of kids at play.

Kids. Darklander cubs, they're called in Mariyad. Not quite like human children, except on the outside.

The children had built a campfire in what had apparently once been a stone altar, now crumbled into an impromptu fireplace. Something about the chant the children were droning stopped us, made us stand in the shadows nearby and watch. The Treflegarian kids wore rags and went barefoot, some of them; others wore fine raiment of imported silk and shiny silver-beaded shoes with upturned toes. The impoverished and the privileged danced together here with an implausible mutual acceptance.

The children were scrawny silhouettes as they danced before the red flames, throwing long, disturbed shadows on the ruins. The smoke seemed to thicken over the dancing children; seemed prompted by their chanting to take on bas-relief definition, figures from the Dark Dimensions shaded in, merely hinted at, then dispelled. Illusions in smoke. Maybe that's all they were.

And then the tallest of the children leapt into the midst of the circle, close beside the fire, and clapped his hands once, hard. The children burst into tittering laughter and scattered, running into the ruins in every direction, squealing excitedly. Tix and I shrank back into the shadows of a crumbling doorway to watch as they played a strange game of hide and seek. A child ran up to a dark archway and gestured with his hand as if releasing a bowling ball—but from his hand came a homunculus, a tiny green leather demon with a spiky head and four claw-tipped arms; the homunculus was no bigger than my hand, but grew knee-high when it struck the ground and then lunged like an elf with rabies into the archway—emerging a moment later chattering nastily, chasing a squealing little girl out into the open where the little boy tagged her and said, "You're it." Poof, she became a homunculus. She was it.

And elsewhere in the ruins we saw children playing leapfrog with actual frogs, frogs big as they were, frogs with glowing silver eyes; we saw children feeding on other children, biting into their limbs with needlelike teeth, tearing the flesh and chewing—but the children who were eaten were laughing the whole time, and minutes later we saw the same kids running by, whole again; and we saw the children hovering in the air, circling one another in a tranced and weightless pavane. We saw twins exchanging heads; they were a boy and a girl, and after exchanging heads they exchanged genitals.

Other children were gathered around a hole in the ground, taking turns reaching in, each pulling out something different: a snake with a crest of fire, writhing into obscene longhand messages; a lava-spitting homunculus covered in scales of jade; a handful of feathers that rearranged to become a miniature, shrieking cave-hawk; a yapping dog that vomited out a tiny laughing clown; a duplicate of one of the other kids, thumbing its nose at the original; a naked female imp with oversized breasts that burst open to disgorge clouds of fireflies; a steaming lump of shit that shivered into a fly-crawling replica of one of the other children, who reacted by reaching into the pit for a snot replica of the one who'd insulted him; another drew out a pair of ordinary novelty-store chattering teeth. Each prize was greeted with gales of laughter and much applause, and then thrown back into the pit. Lastly they drew out miniature writhing figures of . . . we looked closer to be sure. Yes, figures of Tix and Kamus.

The children looked toward us and showed their teeth in wicked grins.

Tix swore and grabbed my arm, dragged us away from there. We found the nearest tavern.

"It's just Darklander kids," I tried to tell him. "It's how they play. They're just goofin' around. Kids will be kids."

But it took two jugs of brew to stop his shaking.

Now, these many years later, I was approaching Treflegar in broad daylight. True, on Ja-Lur broad daylight was no better than Terran twilight. But now that I was adjusted to Ja-Lur it seemed bright out, on the grassy plain.

Certainly it seemed hot. I had another hundred kilometers to go to Treflegar—if indeed that was where the wand would lead me—whereas Buckfinster and Draco had a helicopter and were perhaps a quarter of the way there by now. I toyed with the idea of sending a curse after the copter, making it come unbolted so it fell apart in the air.

But I wasn't sure if all my hypothesizing about those two had been accurate. They were potential sources of information and the detective in me wouldn't let me kill them.

The detective in me. Sometimes I wonder if that could be the literal truth. I'm a sorcerer, too, a dealer in the supernatural; the notion of possession is not a strange one to me. Sometimes it feels as if someone else is in there with me, whispering deductions, hunches . . . Dashiell

113

Hammett worked with the Pinkertons before he was a writer. Maybe it's Hammett.

Probably Hammett's there, whispering to me, but only because I read him, and sometimes when you read a man, he moves into you, and stays.

And whispers, late at night.

I stopped on the plain and shook my head in disgust. My mind was wandering, as I wandered over the plain. Places like this, with a far away horizon, with an unbroken sweep of space around you, lend themselves to strange, introverted ponderings. Places like beaches and plains. And what I needed was some hardcore extroverted action. Something had to be done.

That son of a bitch Sartoris had Andalaya.

And I needed the quantum singularities to get her back. Or so the Darklord claimed.

Walking wasn't going to get me there fast enough. I cast my mind into the air but located no kragor within range. I was sorry I hadn't brought my phonecub. But there was another service I could avail myself of . . .

I was approaching Treflegar, after all. There aren't any more sorcerous towns than dying Treflegar. It should be possible.

I focused my mind on Treflegar, picturing the Dispatch Office. Suddenly it leapt into my mind's eye. A man looked up from his desk, blinking. He was a squat man in a black robe, sitting in a cramped office; behind him was a map of the city and surrounds, and various obscure charts. "This is very rude," he said, glaring at me mentally. "In fact, psychic intrusion is not only rude it's also a misdemeanor. You should use a phonecub or the mail."

"Sorry," I said. "But I haven't got a phonecub, or time to find a mailbox. I'm out in the Sullen Plains, a hundred kilometers from you, on business for the Darklord. I expose my karmic balance sheet for your inspection."

His scowl deepened but he squinted at me—though, in fact, I was nowhere near him, and a visitor to his office would have perceived him as talking to empty air. At last he nodded brusquely. "Very well. You need transportation?"

"The swifter the better."

"I can't authorize interdimensional transfer. And if the Darklord trusted you with it he'd have given you the power to do it yourself."

I ground my teeth in chagrin. He was right. Jann-Togah didn't trust me with instantaneous transportation. Only a few had that power—it could get you into places the Darklord didn't want you, or anyone, to have access to.

"So," the dispatcher continued, "it'll have to be a springfoot."

"No. No no no. No way. A kragor."

"Haven't got one. All dispatched."

"A horse then."

"Haven't got one."

"A donkey."

"They don't exist on Ja-Lur."

"A riding snake."

"Haven't got one."

"A giant bat."

"Haven't got one."

"Magic roller skates?"

"You can have the springfoot."

"Couldn't you conjure something up? A flying demon?"

"Not authorized for that. Conjure it yourself."

"I can't control the damn things, they always try to eat me. How about a giant rat?"

"Haven't got one. You can have a springfoot."

"I can't stand those damn things."

"Neither can anyone else. That's why I've got one left."

I groaned. "Send it."

It nearly stomped me when it arrived.

It was just a dot in the sky at first. Then a blot. Then its shadow fell over me and I threw myself aside and—

BAM!—it came down on its two oversized feet where I'd been standing, bouncing up and down in place on its weirdly spiral-boned legs as they absorbed the kinetic energy. It was big. And it was as ugly as the back end of a dowager with bedsores. It smelled bad and its kind were the most uncomfortable mounts on the planet. It looked like a giant plucked chicken, tall as three men standing on one another, mottled gray and brown, with a chicken head that had droopy lips instead of the chicken beak. It tilted its head at me, looked at me with eyes like wads of phlegm, like it was thinking of chicken-pecking me, and then said in a stupid, droopy voice, "Say uhhhhh, you call for, like, a ride?" It forgot to close its mouth, and drooled. I had to sidestep that, too.

"Yeah. You almost squashed me when you landed, you know."

"Uhhhhhh, oh wow like, sorry, like that's totally grotty. Like, *guy*, I'm sure. I mean, like, what a 'tard, you knoo? I mean, okay?"

"Yeah. Right. Let me on and take me to Treflegar."

It bent over and extended its neck like a suicidal chicken on a chopping block and for a moment I was sorry I didn't have an ax. Then I climbed onto its neck, and as it straightened I slid down to the foam-rubber saddle on its back. I put the wand in the protective bag for fragile items, wishing I could get in with it. I strapped my sword down, put the rubber-band harness on, and sighed, just once, with feeling. I took hold of the creature's loose, rancid neck skin and said, "Go for it."

"Like, fer sure, dude," it said. "Oh wow."

It squatted down as far as it could go on its spring-coil legs—and sprang *up*. Way, way up, *fast*, rocketing into the sky. I was smashed down by acceleration, the wind knocked out of me. The air shrieked past me—and then I was wet. We'd penetrated a cloud. We kept going.

In a moment we broke through the top of the cloud and reached the apex of the leap. We seemed to hang in the air for half a moment as I gasped for air, dreading what was to come. The springfoot gawped stupidly around as we began to fall, admiring the way the silvery light lined the cottony cloud-tops, and said, "Uhhhh, like, wow, that's like *too*-tally rad you knoo?"

And then we were rocketing down through the cloud, falling at an angle, while the springfoot reached under a grimy wing with its fingerlike wingtips, plucked out a fist-sized wad of old well-chewed bubble gum it had kept stuck there, and began to chew it. It blew big, dirty bubbles. And then it *popped* the big, dirty bubbles, with an annoying sound. And blew some more.

The sight put me off gum-chewing. I spat out my own gum into my hand and stuck it on the springfoot's saddle.

"Oh wow, like thanks, I'll, like, have that later, dude," the springfoot said.

And then we hit the ground. I hate that part.

I was smashed down into the saddle by momentum. Or is it inertia? Whatever it was, it had a kick like a mule (whatever a mule is), and the impact made my teeth clack together so hard I had cracks in my molars and my incisors were a centimeter shorter; my joints rattled like dice in a cup. The vertebrae of my spine tumbled one into another like a row of dominoes and my tailbone rang like a cowbell.

It hurt.

And then we were airborne again, the acceleration *G*s smashing me back, the wind knocked out of me.

I was getting a vicious headache. God I hate riding a springfoot.

But each of its jumps took it ten kilometers and after about ten jumps—ten agonizing, skeleton-rearranging, stomach-churning jumps—we were on the outskirts of Treflegar.

"Never again," I muttered, clambering down. "I'm an inch shorter now."

"No extra charge for, like, height adjustment, dude," the springfoot said.

It stared at me as I stretched. "What are you staring

at?'' I demanded, checking to see that my pouch was still there. Also the wand, my sword, and my testicles.

The springfoot said, "I was, just, like, wondering what kind of tip a rad dude like you would, like—"

"Forget it."

"Oh wow. What a dweeb. Like, *too*-tally uncool."

It squatted, broke wind—nearly knocking me over with it—and sprang into the air.

Choking, bones aching, I turned and lurched into Treflegar.

XI

It was sunset. Treflegar was bathed in a halcyon light, all
rusty gold and regal scarlet. The crumbling battlements of
its outer walls were motionless, but I knew there was activity inside.

If you pass through Treflegar, you'll hear people tell
you it's a dying city. You'll hear it so often you'll wish it
would just get it over with and die. But if you say that
aloud, you'll precede it into dissolution.

"Treflegar's a dying city, you know," said an old man,
walking up beside me.

As if on cue, the crumbling battlements crumbled further, a cornice falling away like dried mud from a wheel.
As I passed through the gate, still walking stiffly from the
springfoot ride, the stone gargoyles perched on the walls
glanced at me. One of them picked his nose and yawned.

The old man strolling beside me wore a long dirty gray
robe, patched in places, and an equally patchy and equally
dirty white beard. He had a ski jump nose with a wart on
the end—like the skier perpetually about to make the
jump—and bristling eyebrow. That's eyebrow, singular.
One of them had been ripped away, replaced with a white
scar that showed prominently on his tanned, leathery skin.

"You a traveling salesman?" the old man asked. "A
wand seller?"

I was holding the wand out in front of me, dousing with

119

it, letting it direct me, with minute tugs, to a certain quarter of the city. "No," I said absently, concentrating on the wand. "I'm a detective."

"Defective? That's too bad. Yeah, I can see by the way you're walking, you're a cripple. A beggar, eh? Me too. Charter member of the Beggar's Guild. You going into town to get on the Treflegarian welfare roles? Fat chance. They're real assholes about it. I tried already. It's all political, you know."

He kept tagging along behind me, annoying the hell out of me, as I tried to concentrate on following the wand's signals. We were walking through a torchlit warren of streets heading for the center of Treflegar. The city presented itself to us in high Darklander style. Brooding facades, tortured figures in the carvings; claustrophobia-inducing eaves overhanging streets as crooked as a defense contractor; Ja-Lurian bonsai trees at intervals, the trees shaped to resemble human figures writhing in pain; all the lamps red and purple; the people wearing dark robes with hoods, or faces concealed in garish, psychotic face paint. Crumbling ruins intermixed with high, narrow buildings; mysterious silhouettes in the windows. Ground fog curling over the ancient, cobbled streets; plenty of imported black cats and bats. *You* know the sort of thing. Consciously atmospheric. Treflegar is prone to ground fog but if there isn't any the Utilities department makes some. Good for the tourists.

On one corner a group of city workers brushed some acid onto a cornice so it'd crumble better.

"What we ought to do," the old beggar was saying, "is go to Triangle Square, and get up an act."

"An act?" I asked, trying to be polite.

"Yeah. I'll be your father, see, and you'll be my retarded, crippled son. I'm trying to support you but you're *so retarded* . . ."

"Now look—how about if I'm the son taking care of his doddering, senile father—"

"Don't be absurd, I could never pass for that. Come to

think of it, retarded isn't enough. If we're going to beg, you should probably be hideously deformed, too. Cut off a nose, a limb, that sort of thing. Make them fester with disease. What do you think? Have to make sacrifices for a career, you know. I've got a knife in my robe we could use to make a few minor adjustments in you, nothing you wouldn't live through—"

"Thanks anyway. I think I'll just say, 'Spare Change for Jesus.'"

"Who's Jesus?"

"Never mind."

We had come to the city park. Typical of Darklander parks, it was gloomy, foggy, its forest of contorted, moss-dripping, leafless trees choked with fungus and strangling vines; carnivorous flowers digesting tiny screaming insect-sized humans; here and there were slime-coated ponds rippling with the ominous but ill-defined movement of dark creatures just beneath the surface. From time to time one saw pallid women in diaphanous white gowns laying lilies by gravestones. *You* know the sort of thing.

Nice place. Good landscaping. My Darklander blood sang happily in my veins as I strolled through it. Compositionally all of a piece. I liked the way the moss edging the ponds set off its night-dark surface with just the right degree of hoariness.

That's when I saw them. The Things. I recoiled in disgust.

It was a group of sweet-faced little elves with bells on their toes, dancing in a little fairy circle around what appeared to be butter-yellow daffodils. To my horror, I perceived that tinier, cuter fairies *actually bathed in the dew* caught in the daffodil blossoms.

They all had rosy cheeks and eyes as bright as new buttons.

Ugh. Worse, the little clearing I had stumbled onto was thick with fresh green grass. And a ray of pure white moonlight struck down through the clouds onto a unicorn, a white, shining, silver-horned unicorn, which cropped the green grass. The unicorn was majestic and clean, not even a patch of mange on it.

"My God!" the old man blurted, looking at the elves and flowers and the unicorn. "They've let this place go to Hell in a handbasket!"

I nodded in grave agreement. "Sure looks awful. Really revolting."

"Where's this stuff coming from?"

I didn't answer him, but I had a feeling I knew. The quantum singularity. It'd tapped into the Outfit's most degenerate cultural substrata. At some point in his miserable childhood, Draco—if it was Draco—had been into reading "High Fantasy." They really ought to legislate tougher laws to keep children from getting their hands on this stuff. You think a kid's going to be okay—he's reading de Sade, William Burroughs, Raymond Chandler, Mervyn Peake, Edward Gorey, Lovecraft, Machen, Poe, Hammett; in short, the essentials—but you find out it's a fake book cover. Under that *Naked Lunch* cover is a different book entirely. The kid is reading some unspeakable treacle of an impoverished imagination populated by . . .

By creatures of the sort I was seeing before me now. Unicorns. Elves. Fairies with transparent wings. Friendly, talking owls.

Along came a nauseatingly beautiful blond princess with her hair up in some kind of pinhead cone, her big blue eyes laughing as she blew kisses to the little bluebirds who twittered around her golden tresses. The dimples in her rosy cheeks were emitting little valentines. "Tra la la," she sang. "Tra la la!"

I was in a Darklander city, and the Darklander blood in me was fired up; my Darklander sensibility was foremost. The Earth half of me was dormant. So I reacted to the sight of this abomination as a Darklander would.

I admit it: The horror overcame me—and I screamed. I'm as tough as any guy, but the sight of this prancing princess with the impossibly clean little white feet was too much even for a hardnosed private dick.

I screamed and ran.

But there was more. I found myself panting on the edge of another moonlit clearing where a knight in glimmering argent, with a shield the color of the light on a morning sea, stood gazing austerely into the distance, his long golden tresses blowing around his finely chiseled face. His regular features beaming with nobility, simplicity, and inspired purpose. Beside him was his silver-maned stallion, likewise caparisoned in shining armor.

A stomach-twisting sight, let me tell *you.*

The knight looked at me with distaste. So did his horse. He smiled wearily, as if resigning himself to consorting with people from the wrong side of the tracks, and asked, "I say, fellow, have you seen in yon forest a maiden fair?"

"Yeah—"

"Answer not hastily. There are many fair maidens but the one I seek is above all others. Her eyes are the blue of an Alpine sky on a summer morn; her hair is more golden than all the treasure of Croesus; her hands are like the twinkling at the edge of stars—"

"Yeah yeah and her gown is a copy of a Paris designer original," I growled. "I saw her. She was heading for the unicorn. He seemed interested in her. She was eyeing his horn. She's probably riding him gaily through the woods."

"I don't believe I like the tone you use in talking of the fair Lady Klonessa," he began, the glint in his eyes matching that of the sword he now drew from its silver mesh scabbard.

"Look, the bitch made me sick, okay? I need an insulin shot after seeing her. The little miss prig doesn't belong here."

"What . . . did . . . you . . . call *HER*?!" He brandished his sword so it flashed in the moonlight. "Come, you blackguard, and draw your sword! We fight to the death!"

"Oh, fuck *off,*" I said, and went back into the woods.

He didn't pursue me. Probably he was occupied with the fearsome but gem-resplendent dragon who'd huffed down into the clearing, looking fully as magnificent and picturesque as the knight. The dragon had a big leather-bound book in one of his claws and a condescending look in his eyes. One thing I hate, it's intellectual dragons.

I turned my back on them both and slipped away through the woods, following the tug of the seeking wand, which led me to yet another nauseating set piece.

Dwarves, ten of them, the sort with kelly-green medieval outfits, peaked hats, long white beards, and lines from smiling and wisdom on their gruff-but-friendly faces.

They were planting magical trees, or something. Little white-boughed saplings. They looked up at me with delight and sardonic twinklings in their little eyes. "He is here!" their leader declared, tugging on an earlobe and winking. "He who is Chosen for the Quest."

I looked around. "You mean me?"

"Tee hee hee," this adorable rabble laughed. "Ho ho ho! 'You mean me?!' he says! Indeed we do, for the Lady of the Willows awaits you in the sacred grove of—"

"Hey bull-*shit* pal!" I told him, backing away.

"Ho ho! Tee hee!" they said, coming toward me, eyes twinkling merrily. God what a revolting sight.

I was mesmerized by their cuteness. Paralyzed. About to be drawn into their meaningless imperatives.

When suddenly a man leapt from the bushes. He had a gray cap and a gray jumpsuit and a tank on his back connected to a little hose held in his hand. On his shoulder was a patch that said, CITY OF TREFLEGAR PEST CONTROL. He sprayed the dwarves with a pesticide mist and they all fell dead.

"Thank God," I said, enormously relieved.

"Yes," he said. "You really ought to stay out of the park. There's a problem with the little buggers. Nauseating, treacly stuff of all kinds underfoot all over the park."

"I'll split as soon as I can," I said. "Listen—there's a

knight in armor with a dragon and a beautiful maiden back there where I just came from—"

He made a face. "You'd think I'd get used to the nasty things." He sighed. "I'm not really cut out for this. Haven't got the stomach for the sight of them. Well, I'd better get to it. Dragon and knight you say? Beautiful maiden?" He shook his head in disgust and went in the direction I'd indicated.

"Keep up the good work!" I called after him, with complete sincerity.

I wish I'd persuaded him to stick with me. I went on my way and not fifty meters on I stumbled into another pack of elves. These were cuter than the first I'd seen. They beamed at me—literally, light coming out of their eyes in welcome—and where they danced flowers sprang up. They had upturned noses. And with them was another tribe of vermin—*smurfs*. Little blue guys with floppy hats and naked feet. Their outlines kind of vague and clunky, as if they'd been badly drawn. Smurfs! Enough to make a man lose his lunch.

They were dancing around me, singing little songs of welcome.

I reached into my memory, and found some Darklore. I smiled nastily. I chanted.

The dark energies quivered up from deep underground, entered the soles of my feet, and left me through my hands. Sensing what was coming down, the smurfs and elves tried to run. But it was too late. The dark energies swirled around them, paralyzed them in place, and the transformation took effect. The elves shrieked as their cute oversized limpid brown eyes began to wriggle in their sockets and then popped out, revealing themselves to be the glossy brown heads of worms that wagged obscenely from side to side even as the elves' ears became longer, pointier, dirtier, scabby, and tufted with bristles; pig snouts replaced their cute little noses, and fangs replaced their pearly teeth. Their hands became gnarly and grew claws; claws burst through their bell-tipped shoes; their backs grew hunched and their muscles swelled brutishly. They'd become nasty, carnivorous trolls. Darklandish creatures.

"Now that's more like it," I said, turning and slipping off to the woods. Once safely in the woods I released the former elves from their paralysis.

I didn't have to transform the smurfs. Because the trolls simply ate them.

The wand led me to an annoyingly symmetrical grove of luminous silver willow trees. I was distantly aware that the old beggar who'd followed me earlier had cropped up again and was trailing me about twenty meters back. It bothered me, but I was concentrating on other things.

Like the Lady of the Willows.

She was tall, exquisitely elegant in her iridescent gown of flowing waters; she was very finely boned, her hair the color of her gown except for a streak of black, her eyes changing color, now blue-purple, now cat's-eye, her expression infinitely gentle but terrible to look at for its burden of ancient wisdom; her features ageless and yet somehow inclusive of all ages of Woman.

Also, she had a nice dimple in her chin.

Good figure, too. Double D cups, at least.

I didn't whistle, though. I was tempted, but I didn't. Because around her neck on a leather thong was a crystal, a raw chunk of quartz, and in it was the oscillating non-shape of a quantum singularity.

"Where are they *getting* these leather thongs and crystals?" I muttered. "It doesn't go with the rest of her look."

I saw also, as I approached her, that her gown was flowing out of *her* in some way, a gown of liquid that flowed ceaselessly onto the ground, breaking up into little streams that meandered with conscious purpose into the surrounding woods . . .

And somehow, out there, helped create the elves, the dwarves, the other cuteness atrocities.

I was at the source of the pestilence. I considered heading back to find the City Exterminator but decided against it. She was probably too powerful for pesticides.

"So," she said, her voice resonating like the wind in the trees and the echo of brooks along wooded hillsides and all that sort of thing, "you have come to take up your quest."

"Uh, actually, lady, not to be rude," I said, "I've come to suggest you go back to your own dimension of reality. The singularity you wear around your neck brought you to our dimension by accident, because of your attunement with the degenerate minds of the Outfit, who like to escape to that kind of fantasy, see. They like to fantasize simplistic stuff, cheerful formula stuff, get their morality ya-yas out that way, so that when they come back to the real world they can get away with murder, and every kind of irresponsibility. Also, they have bad taste. That's my theory, anyway. And your presence here is a real administrative and sanitation problem, you know? It's worse than cleaning up a stadium after a Superbowl. Causing real problems locally."

She gazed at me pityingly. "Foolish one, I am here by no accident. The Lady dances to the choreography of the gods."

"Yeah. Right. But—"

"I am here to bring light to this dark place."

"But see, lady, we don't *want* it. We *like* it gloomy. I mean, the whole world has a hangover all the time, you know? Bright lights hurt the eyes, makes the headache throb. Forget it."

"Once you are on the Quest, you will see."

"Uh *huh*." The only thing left to do was play along. Get a little closer with the wand. "Okay. I guess you got me."

She smiled. A smile like the first sunshine of the spring.

I needed an aspirin. Make it Alka-Seltzer, something for the stomach, too.

I moved closer to her. "So, uh, what's the assignment?" I asked.

"In the mountains to the East, there is a great cave, all of blue ice. Within it resides an ogre. He is terrible, hideous to look upon, but he was not always so."

"I know the feeling. On the day I turned thirty-two I noticed I had—"

I broke off, seeing she was looking at me reproachfully. I shrugged apologetically and took a step closer. She went on, "This ogre is called Schprechstaffle." She said this with a distinctly Bavarian accent. "He guards a treasure that can restore to this world a springtime long denied it, a golden rose. Win past this ogre—and the Secret Monstrosities who surround him—and bring the rose to me. When my sacred waters fall upon the rose, its like will bloom over all the world, giving out the sunlight your world lacks, and ushering in a new age."

"Sounds good. I'll get right on it." I made a mental note to tell the Darklord to check out this ogre and have him simply put some herbicide on the golden rose forthwith.

I had edged close enough. The wand in my hand was vibrating eagerly. A sudden look of hurt and suspicion came into the Lady's eyes—and for a moment I felt a pang of sorrow and regret. I admit it.

Fortunately, I belched and the regret was gone. And then the singularity was sucked out of the crystal around the Lady's neck and into the wand. It hummed for a moment in satiated satisfaction.

The lady moaned and shrank into herself, then drained away into a crack in the ground. In seconds she was gone. More fragile than the boss of the jet-skiers, apparently.

I looked around. The willows were gone, too. In their place were some crooked trees and a hangman's gallows, creaking in the rising storm. It began to rain; a chill, bitter rain. A raven croaked at me from the gallows where it perched on the skull of the skeleton swinging slowly in the wind.

I inhaled deeply and said, "Ahhhhh."

Now that was more like it.

I was beat. Really tired. I'd done magic, and I'd faced an army of lethal saccharinity, and now I wanted rest. I headed for an inn I knew on the eastern edge of the city park, a place called The Final Rest.

I had just reached the street when the old beggar caught up with me. "Look," I said, "I'm bushed. I'm just not into this beggar stuff. I have another career in mind. I was thinking maybe I could learn word processing, or I could be an insurance actuary. I heard they get a good wage."

"You're quite sure?" He took a step closer, smiling. "Well, if that's what you want . . . You have my blessings!" Another step closer.

Where had I just seen this keep-them-talking-while-edging-closer-and-then-make-your-move gag?

Ah. I'd just done it myself.

I put my hand on my sword, but it was too late. He had already grabbed the wand and was beginning to change his aspect. He wasn't what he appeared to be.

He was some kind of demon, and it looked to be one of the more mean-tempered breeds.

XII

The demon had grabbed the wand. I mentioned that. I forgot to mention, though, that I'd refused to let go of it on my end.

So he was dangling me over the ground.

He was about four meters high, and shaped like a termite from the neck down. A termite big enough to chew through a forest alone. From the neck up was a head bristling with tusks and tendrils, fangs and barbs—but there were no eyes. It was a head neither insect nor human. But somehow I felt it glaring at me as it lifted me up toward its mouth with one pincer, while the other snapped teasingly at my belly, snipping away buttons on my shirt.

This trip was not exactly a Hawaiian vacation.

I began to chant—and it spat in my face. It spat a malodorous, sticky white paste that instantly hardened and glued my mouth shut. I gagged, and I couldn't speak, and the spell died in my throat.

The demonic pincers took me by the neck—oh yes, I was trapped, choking again—and shook me a few times, as it laughed with a sound like a Siamese cat going mad.

And then it spoke. But not to me.

"I have him, Sartoris." Speaking in the ancient tongue of the Darklanders. *"What would you have me do with him? May I feed him to my children?"*

"He would only suffer a few days that way," Sartoris said.

His face had appeared in a whirling black cloud above us. He was not there in person; was still in his distant fortress, probably.

And yet he was looking down at me, chuckling, the red light from his eyes sunburning their imprint on my forehead. "I will take him and enter his brain, in the form of a virus, and I will wreak a havoc there like the destruction of ten thousand worlds. For there are ten thousand worlds in every man's brain, Kamus of Kadizhar, and you will suffer each of them."

I couldn't speak, so I gave him the finger.

"Whatever peculiar magical sign that is," Sartoris said, "it is futile. It will not save you." He was right about that, anyway. "Now, Vindick," Sartoris told the demon, "take the black holes from him and render him to me through the turnstile of the seventeenth dimension, on the Uptown side of the station."

"Couldn't I at least take a bite out of him?" Vindick asked. *"Just a bite, and then I'll send him along? He'll still be alive. I won't touch his brain, I promise."*

"Oh, very well."

Sartoris vanished. In his place was a doorway that had appeared in midair. It was a graffitti-covered thing of tile and concrete with the sign, Subway Entrance. It looked ominous. The demon raised me to its mouth . . .

But then a roar and a honking and a screech of tires and a billow of exhaust announced the entry of another factor into the equation. Both the demon and I stared in amazement at the new arrival.

It was a 1966 Ford Mustang convertible, powder blue, chopped, channeled, and with headers. Whitewall tires.

"What manner of spirit is this?" the demon Vindick wondered aloud.

There were two guys in the car. That's all I saw before it plowed into the demon's lower parts, knocking it off its hind legs, so it sprawled backwards across the hood. It let go of me and the wand in its pain and confusion, and I rolled to the side, then vaulted into the back of the car as it swung around. I still had the wand. The demon Vindick got to its feet again, trying to block the escape of the Mustang convertible. The man in the passenger side of the front seat was smoking an ordinary briar pipe; now he took it from his mouth and pointed the stem at the outraged demon—and lightning licked out of the pipe stem, blasting the demon into steaming chunks of insect gel. The head rolled away on the ground, snarling in fury.

The car did a U-ey and burned rubber. We barreled out of there.

The car's driver reached back and, looking at me only in the rearview mirror, grabbed the glue pasting my mouth shut. All at once he ripped it away.

"Yeee-OWW!" was my response. But it was gone, just like ripping away a Band-Aid, and it didn't take any skin with it. Not much, anyway.

"No need to thank me," the stranger said.

The blue Mustang convertible careened through the twisty streets of Treflegar, and then suddenly we were through the gate and out on the open road, headed southwest, into the plains and into the moon-haunted night. The driver switched on the headlights and for a moment I thought I was back on Earth, driving through a Texan desert, blindly following the sleepwalker's arms of the headlights into the darkness. I expected to see a jackrabbit stare glassily into the lights up ahead, and maybe an armadillo or two.

But it was Ja-Lur, and the only fauna I saw was a tumblebug and a hopping snake. Somewhere overhead, a kragor screeched mournfully.

The wand in my hand told me we were moving in the right direction. But was I going there with the right people? Were these the ones Jann-Togah had mentioned? Slim Shim and Slam Sham?

The two guys in the front seat were prosaic-looking humans. They were Earthmen, so far as I could tell, but not dressed like men of the current age. The driver was a short, stocky fellow with dark, wavy, swept-back hair, a pleasantly pinched face, and small eyes. He wore blue jeans, a tattered Levi jacket, and horn-rim glasses. He was smoking a cigarette; the stuff in the cigarette was not tobacco.

I'd smelled that smell before, amongst certain wizards. It was the sacred herb, frop.

The other fellow was smoking the same thing. He was tall, with the impossibly regular features you see on a mannequin; his black hair was combed back from his forehead with an excess of hair oil. His face, all the time I knew him, was one expression. He was grinning. He was always grinning. Usually with the pipe—also burning the sacred herb—clamped in his teeth.

He turned to me and stuck out his hand. We shook hands. "Name's 'Bob'!" He said. You could hear the quotation marks around the name. "J.R. 'Bob' Dobbs! I'm in sales!"

"You're not . . . uh—Slim Shim?" I asked. "The Darklord said—"

"Sure, sure I am! Or anyway, I'm Slam Sham! My friend here is Slim Shim! We go by those names when we work as a team." He was still shaking my hand. It was getting sweaty. He grinned at me, his eyebrows arched. He never blinked. His eyes were real eyes, but he never blinked them.

I took my hand back and said, "If your real name isn't Slam Sham—then I'm guessing that his isn't really Slim Shim. So what is it?"

"His name? It's Stang. That's the good Reverend Ivan Stang! As faithful a puppy as ever soiled a newspaper!" "Bob" said, slapping Stang on the shoulder.

"Don't fuck with me, 'Bob,'" Stang snarled. Stang was driving with one hand but not noticeably watching where he was going. He was bent over the dashboard, fiddling testily with the car radio, squinting his eyes against smoke from the hand-rolled cigarette. Nothing but raucous squawks came out of the radio. "Shit for radio on this planet," he muttered. "You want a hit of this here frop?"

"No thanks. It makes me paranoid, or sleepy. Where'd you get the car?" I asked.

"We found it in a used car lot," Stang said. "Up at the third singularity locus. You'll see when you get there. Things like this cropping up all over. Darklord sent us along to help you through it. He's paying us in Slack Bonds."

"How come the Darklord picked a couple of Earthmen for this?" But then, remembering "Bob"'s lightning-charged pipe, I realized my mistake. "You guys are wizards?"

"Is the pope Catholic?" "Bob" said, cheerfully.

"We're Earthmen," Stang said, "but not all Earthmen are really Earthmen." He spoke with a faint Texas accent. The cigarette clamped in his lips waggled with each word, spilling ashes into his lap. "Your Darklord, now, he picked us because we understand the nature of this particular kind of metaphysical infection. What you call the Outfit. We call it the Conspiracy." The car bounced as it went over a hump that marked the edge of an asphalt road. There were no asphalt roads on Ja-Lur. But we'd driven onto one, somehow, anyway. Up ahead was a cluster of harsh white lights; their cruel brilliance told me they were electric lights. Stang went on, "The Conspiracy's mindset is perverting your planet. We've been chippin' away at the Con on Earth, in our own time." He glanced over his shoulder at me and added casually, "Besides being space travelers, we're time travelers, too. I forgot to tell you that."

He wasn't looking where he was going, and we hit the oil slick full bore.

It was a big, black, gas-rainbowed oil slick in the middle of the asphalt road, and the car spun out on it, spinning as if on a turntable three times and then sliding sideways. And stopped. The engine coughed and died.

And then they had surrounded us.

There were maybe fourteen of them, Earthmen or Ja-Lurians with serious Earth-damage, crowding around the car with guns in their hands. They smoked real cigarettes. They wore designer sunglasses, and designer jeans, and designer tennis shoes. The sunglasses were understandable, though it was night, because all around us were the sources of the harsh electric shine I'd seen earlier, "anti-crime" streetlights on steel poles, equally powerful lights over the doorways of the ugly buildings crowding the street to either side. There were telephone poles and power poles with wires strung like web from a disorganized spider, and there were big plastic molded signs like DEEP-FRIED LEFTOVERS and GET-IT-QUIK LIQUOR and PIONEER CHICKEN—easily the ugliest sign I'd ever seen, with a cockeyed chef sitting on a badly drawn covered wagon, the whole an anticomposition that could have been in the dictionary under "eyesore"—and PORK PARTS! PORK PARTS MEANS FAST EATS RIGHT NOW NOW NOW!

My heart sank. The transformation had already taken hold.

We were too late.

"Okay," said one of the men, gesturing with the big black gun in his hand. "Out of the car." He was wearing a T-shirt printed with DO IT WITH DIPPY DOG! DRINK DIPPY DOG BEER! There was a picture of a rather anthropomorphic dog winking as it swilled a can of beer.

"What happens after we get out of the car?" I asked. The wand in my hand was tugging to the Southwest. I'd learned to interpret its dousing signals. It was saying the singularity wasn't here—though this place had to be an effect of the last singularity—it was farther down the road.

"What happens is," the Dippy Dog guy said, "we take this here real nice car for me to drive, and then we take

135

you to the Big Computer what puts you through your paces and makes you into one of us. You'll be Outfit through and through, and you'll like it. Or, we kill you. You wouldn't like that.''

"Sorry boys!" "Bob" said cheerfully, his grin never wavering, the pipe wagging in his teeth, "Can't oblige you."

The Dippy Dog guy pointed his pistol at "Bob"'s head and cocked it. "Then kiss your ass good-bye."

"Mind if we pray first?" "Bob" asked, still smiling.

The Dippy Dog guy hesitated. "I guess not. Make it quick. You do a quick prayer—unless you're going to try some kinda Darkland-type wizard hocus pocus and pray to some gawddamn demon."

"Nope!" Stang said. "We're gonna pray to Jesus!"

"Jesus?" The Dippy Dog guy said. He shrugged. "He's harmless. Go ahead."

I stared at them in disbelief. They were going to pray to . . . to *Jesus*?!

Stang looked up at the sky. "Jesus, I'd sure appreciate it if you'd kinda drop in and escort those who're deservin' through yore pearly gates. Or whichever gates you deem appropriate."

"Okay, enough praying," the Dippy Dog guy said. He aimed the gun at "Bob"'s forehead.

And then he blinked and looked up, distracted by a light in the sky.

A ball of soft luminescence was descending the sky, coming down directly overhead, straight and true as an elevator. In fact, it *was* an elevator, a shining elevator without a building, and when it opened, five meters over the road, a man leapt out of it.

More than a man. It was Jesus. Jesus—with a submachine gun in His hand and a burning cigar clamped in his mouth. When I say Jesus, I mean Jesus.

I don't mean Jesus Garcia of Western Avenue, East L.A. I mean *Jesus*. Of Nazareth. He had the crown of thorns, he had the stigmata, he had the beard, he had the robe and sandals, he had the halo.

He also looked sore as Hell. And he had that submachine gun in his hand aimed downward.

His leap out of the elevator carried him to the air in front of it—but he didn't fall, he hovered up there, opening up with the machine gun.

That's right. The submachine gun rattled in Jesus' hands, barking murderous firepower, blasting the Dippy Dog guy into kiblets, blowing away a half dozen more of the Outfit thugs, the submachine gun shaking him with its recoil, the cigar almost bitten in half in his angrily clenched teeth. Jesus was yelling through those clenched teeth, "Yeeeeee-*haw*!"

I knew him, then. He wasn't merely "Jesus." I'd read about *this* Jesus in the Sacred Scroll of Hypercryptic Ikons: He wasn't your ordinary Jesus. He was . . .

THE *FIGHTIN'* JESUS!

And the sight of the Fightin' Jesus blazing away up there was inspiring as all Hell. I had ducked down between the front and the backseats, staying out of it, but I was inspired by the sight.

Meanwhile, "Bob" had let loose the lightnings of his terrible swift pipe, electrocuting two more of the thugs, while Stang used their confusion to stomp the accelerator and get us out of there, with deft jerks of the steering wheel smashing a couple of Outfit mind-clones out of the way, using the car as his club. "Have to get those damn fenders replaced from a gawddamn junk yard, can't get parts for the sixty-six no more," he complained, as we roared down the road.

Behind us, the Fightin' Jesus was turning back to the elevator. He'd killed all the thugs who hadn't run. Now he punched the buttons on the elevator, waited till the door opened. He turned and made a gesture of benediction toward us, then a breezy salute of camaraderie. He stepped into the shining lift and rode it back to the stars.

I got up and leaned back in the seat. Realizing I was tired. Tired but impressed. "Man, you guys have got *connections*!"

I must've slept. Something I was long overdue for.

When I woke it was dawn, and we were driving through a nightmare.

All around us, the worst of two hundred years of Earth Kulture had flowered into being, in its most egregious manifestations. For two hundred years the imperatives that gave rise to the Outfit—the Conspiracy to exploit the Earth and all its people like a combination hot dog and souvenir stand on Coney Island—had dominated portions of the Earth. Some of the Earth was controlled by the Unity powers—relatively enlightened, environmentally balanced, civilized but not insanely growth-oriented. But much of Earth still belonged to the multinationals, and the crime/business cartels. The Outfit. And the Outfit was a state of mind.

And the landscape of that mind had superimposed itself over the landscape of Ja-Lur.

The taste we'd had of it back at the town where the Fightin' Jesus had pulled our chestnuts from the fire—that was nothing, compared to this.

The first town had been sprawled to either side of the road; essentially based on one surface, the horizontal one. But this, now . . .

My stomach worked itself into the whole lexicon of Boy Scout knots as I looked around in disgust. Because the stuff was everywhere. It was to the right, the left, to the front and back, it was diagonal, and it was straight overhead. Everywhere but underneath. Under us was asphalt. The town-tube went on as far as I could see, ahead and behind. We'd driven into a hive of urban sprawl and over-development, with countless discount stores, fast food joints, convenience stores, sheep's hide car-seat cover shops, motels built with all the design sense of a beehive hairdo, new and used car lots, remaindered furniture outlets, gas stations, drive-thru banks, drive-thru churches, drive-thru massage parlors, drive-thru funeral homes, drive-thru restaurants, drive-thru liquor stores, drive-thru dentistry, drive-thru gland transplants, drive-thru wedding chapels, drive-thru facial rearrangement clinics, drive-thru golf courses.

And there were donut shops, too. We stopped at a *Dunkin' Donuts* for coffee and bear claws. They weren't real bear claws. That's just what they call them.

The donut shop was upside down.

It was suspended upside down directly over the street, like a garish chandelier on the ceiling of the great tunnel the street had become. To either side were a dry cleaner, a franchise from a hairdresser called *Johnny Cutter's,* and various pizza dealerships. All of them upside down, or projecting out sideways from some hidden wall. It was as if they'd taken three business-crowded streets and laid them out to the side and overhead in the shape of an infinitely elongated coffin. We were on the inside of the coffin lid, eating bear claws.

We were upside down, but it didn't feel that way, and there was no gravitational problem. Don't ask me how they pulled that off. To the quantum singularity the laws of physics were as changeable as the hair color of a disco queen.

We could see the car parked on the street down below us—only, it looked like it was suspended over our heads.

I sipped my coffee and looked out through the smog-grimed plastic window at this M. C. Escherian scene, with people walking down the sides of walls, on the narrow walkways between the shops, and then across a street that was a ceiling to us, and then down—or up, depending on where you were—the other side. Back to our plane of reference. Everyone—dressed roughly like the men who'd attacked us on the outer town—was in a hurry, was checking a watch, was swearing at someone else for causing a delay in a line. Everyone here was too involved in their activity to attack us—caught up in the maddening pursuit of some illusion; some psychological carrot hanging before their sociobiological donkey.

"Bob," Stang, and I were immune to whatever psychic force field was tugging these people, dragging them like little metal-based men pulled on an electric football game. Stang had exhibited a feverish purposefulness in driving all night to get here, but he was moving according to his own agenda—not one superimposed by the Outfit. Somehow I sensed that "Bob" himself was the source of the immunity. He seemed to emanate the essence of the easygoing, moving through things with the sluggish grace of melting wax. He was some kind of super-Taoist, "Bob" was—maybe possessed by the Tao principle itself. He went with the flow and yet, when the time was right, he directed his movements in it. He gave off a kind of transparent radiation of what he called Slack—which is what he said the Outfit specialized in stealing from the rest of us. Slack. Our freedom to do as we damned pleased.

The human automatons ran feverishly from one meaningless task to another—going to the pizza shop to get food, spilling the food on their shirts, taking the shirts frantically to the dry cleaner, getting their hair disarranged by a fan in the dry cleaner which meant they had to, simply *had* to, go to a hairdresser, need money for the hairdresser, have to stop at an instant teller, not enough money, work in the bank to pay for the money from the bank, then pay for the hairdresser, pay for the dry cleaning, go to a video arcade to "relax" with a series of violent onscreen encounters, get hungry from all this so get a pizza, spill the pizza on the shirt, go to the drycleaner to get the shirt clean, get your hair disarranged at the drycleaner so you have to go to the hairdresser . . .

And they did this thinking they were doing it by choice.

Sitting with "Bob" I felt protected from all this evil magic. "Bob" was a psychic rock protecting me from a chilling wind. I sat comfortably in his lee, sipping coffee.

He smiled at me, and he told the waitress I would pay for the donuts.

As we looked out the window, we saw other people just arriving, puzzled Ja-Lurians coming in on carts and beasts of burden—that were immediately confiscated by the police to be used in making burgers—and quickly mesmerized by the feverish activity and the poisonous psychic emanations of the plastic signs and lights and video displays. They were herded into lines and marched down the streets to a sort of high-tech art-deco temple.

Stang, "Bob," and I left the donut shop to investigate.

Minutes later we had joined the crowd of newcomers being ushered into the temple. We played along, looking glassy-eyed and bleating from time to time.

It looked like a sleek, chrome and tile, yuppified late twentieth-century version of the Ziggurat of Zoln. Instead of Zoln's figures of people writhing in hellfire torment, the outside was decorated with neatly painted bas-relief figures of people working out in body building spas and toasting in tanning parlors and boiling in hot tubs and jogging. Utopia's own fires of torment.

Inside we were ushered into a great hall reeking with the mingled scents of sweat, deodorant, aftershave, and blood.

The walls were banks of television screens, each tuned to a different channel. The walls showed a forever changing tapestry of video imagery drawn from old Earth, most of it from the late twentieth century, early twenty-first, the height of the era Unity historians now refer to as The Great Embarrassment.

Most of the channels were feverish with violence. Itchy with emotionless sex. Glittery with glossy products. Bland with superficial analysis.

But all that was a lot of strobing on the periphery of my attention. I'd only glanced at it. There was something more sinister occupying the center of the room.

In the center of the room was the Boss of the Blue Arrow tribe.

XIII

He had changed, in some ways. In other ways he was just more of the same.

The Boss was bigger, and his fittings were more articulated. The great three-story-high bulk of his metal-pyramid body was decked out with circuit boards and chip boards and Monopoly boards. Here and there in cracks between the boards were sections of human flesh gone gray and puffed out like vinyl around the buttons on a seat cushion.

From the boards on the Boss's sides extruded a fine beard of fiber optic hairs that connected to goggles; the goggles were fitted by armed attendants in orange chain-restaurant-type uniforms onto the new inductees. The inductees were lined up along both sides of the room, staring at stacks of hundreds of TV screens. The goggles were multifaceted, bug-eye things; somehow, I suspected, the fiber optics and goggles enabled the new inductee to watch all the TVs at once . . .

They stood there shaking from the overdose, the input of mass quantities of stylized information.

The head of the Boss, way up there on the apex of the metal and flesh pyramid, had the same features—but expressing a mercurial shifting between rage, leering delight, sick horror, and orgasmic abandon, remaining only seconds in each expression. It was sickening to watch; sickening as the smell from the Great Out-House of Holovan.

Sometimes, after looking ecstatic for a moment, the Boss retched and vomited. Then looked enraged, and then revoltingly happy. And then sick again.

Every so often an attendant on a scaffold swabbed the pyramid of vomit and phlegm.

Below the scaffold was the great, horrible mouth I had seen before, unchanged except that now it took in a new tribe of victims. Anyone who resisted the goggles—and a few did, despite the psychic undertow of the place—were fed into that enormous slobbering mouth.

"The belly of the Beast," Stang muttered, sliding a hand into his coat. I glimpsed the butt of a .44 under his hand.

I looked for the last singularity, expecting to see it on a thong around the Boss's neck. But it wasn't there. He'd learned his lesson about leaving it out in the open.

I knew he had it, though. Partly because of the wand—but also because of his psychic enslavement of these people. The singularity gave him that power. He had been brought here—or in some way had brought himself here—because, I supposed, he was the embodiment of the Outfit, and the singularity was reflecting the mindset of the Outfit. Chances were, it had been impregnated with that mindset when it was stolen by them. Hojas Mor had overridden the Outfit's influence with his own psychic influence. With the masking power of Hojas gone, the singularity broke out in sores from the underlying infection.

I stopped ruminating and started thinking defense strategy. *You're in serious jeopardy here, twerp,* I told myself. I checked out the boss again.

From time to time, between retchings, the Boss hungrily scanned the crowd, looking with a mixture of anticipation and fury for signs of resistance on their faces. I ducked my face behind a tall woman wearing the furry hat of a nomad, hoping it would block the boss's view of me. I had no wish for him to recognize me. Stang, "Bob," and I were about forty people back in the double row of inductees. The ones at the front were taken two at a time to the

143

goggles. Or to the mouth. In a few minutes we'd have the same choice. The devil or the deep blue sea.

Yeah. Blue is the color of television light. A light you can drown yourself in.

I didn't wonder how the great bulk of the Boss had been moved here. Obviously the singularity was capable of world-class wonders. Obviously the late Hojas Mor had only just tapped the surface of the potential in the Black Hole of Carcosa.

Thinking of Hojas made me think of Andalaya. I felt like someone had shoved a long hat pin into the soft place under my sternum.

Keep your hands off her, Sartoris. Keep your thoughts off of her. Keep away from her, you bastard.

With luck, I told myself, Sartoris was occupied with searching for me. "Bob"'s peculiar, invisible emanations protected me from Sartoris's sorcerous searching—or so Stang had assured me—but eventually "Bob" would have to T.C.O.B back on Earth. (In fact, "Bob" had a tattoo, he told me, that worked "T.C.O.B." into a nice design. Take Care Of Business. Or maybe "Take Care Of 'Bob.'" I asked to see the tattoo and, grinning, he started to unzip his pants—I told him to forget it.)

Eventually, I'd be on my own again. And then Sartoris would scent me out. Send his supernatural bloodhounds after me. Well, I'd flush that bilge when I came to it.

As we got closer to the Boss, I noticed two other things. An arrow—a blue arrow—stuck in the flesh between circuit boards, near the top of the pyramid. Well short of his head, the only part of him conceivably vulnerable to a small weapon. My acquaintance among the jet-skiers had tried to kill the boss and failed.

The other observation was the pipelines coming out of his base, feeding into the walls. They were metal—but they throbbed with a pulse and exuded a glow of both ions and heat energy.

I remembered the Lady of the Willows. The water flowing with impossible endlessness out of her flesh, into the gown that became streams feeding into the woods, infecting the place with virulent kitsch. These rootlike pipes had to be something of the same phenomenon . . . The pipes were creating the fake city around the temple . . . Seeding it, feeding it, harvesting from it . . .

Now if I could just locate the singularity.

I had the wand concealed under my coat, one hand on it just as Stang kept one hand on his gun. I could feel it trembling, pulling now irresistibly, shoving out of my coat—prodding the woman in front of me from behind.

"Please," she said, turning to me, "control your carnal impulses."

I looked down and saw the way the wand was pushing out my coat from inside. "Oh. Sorry. It's not what it . . . I mean . . ." But she'd snorted contemptuously and turned away—after stepping prudently to one side.

I glanced over my shoulder. And felt a chill. Draco and Buckfinster were just six places back in line. They were entirely under the boss's influence, as far as I could tell. This was where their search for the singularity had led them. Slavery.

I looked to the front—and swallowed, hard. We were the second-to-next in line.

I could smell the rot from the Boss's giant undermouth; could hear the muffled screams as someone was crushed in its jaws. Could see the others being led away, in a curious sort of natural selection, to be fitted with goggles.

I looked at "Bob." I shook my head in incredulity.

He showed no anxiety whatsoever. His expression hadn't changed. He was humming a little tune. I think it was "The Girl From Ipanema." Stang was smiling too, a grim smile that went with the glitter in his flinty little eyes.

But we were going to be next.

I'd come in expecting I'd see the third singularity, grab it, and, in the general chaos, escape.

No singularity. Nothing.

I cleared my throat. "Stang," I whispered. "You got a plan?"

145

"Yeah. After all this is over I thought I'd go back to Texas, get my family, take us on a nice vacation. I was thinking maybe Mexico, I know a nice place on the Gulf Coast where they sell—"

"That's not what I mean, dammit!" I hissed.

The attendants came and took the people ahead of us. We were next. Six meters ahead was the mouth.

"We could run for it," "Bob" suggested cheerfully.

"We'd never get ten feet," I said. "How about the Fightin' Jesus?"

"He's on break."

"How about using the lightning in your pipe?"

"Wrong polarity here. The pyramid fellow is well insulated. He'd just absorb the power." He didn't seem even remotely worried; he puffed blissfully on his pipe as, a few meters away, the giant mouth champed in anticipation of us. "Some pyramid, eh? I had a pyramid scheme myself, once, back in 1952, it was, and I remember—"

In desperation, as the attendants approached us, I pulled the wand into the open and let it have its head.

It pointed into the Boss's mouth. The big one.

The hungry one. The stinking, bloody, slavering one. I glimpsed the singularity then, as that mouth opened wide for us. It was sunk into the flesh at the back of the throat.

Oh, no.

Maybe "Bob" was right. There was something to be said for running.

I thought about Andalaya. I sighed. I said, "Distract them with the gun, Stang, I'm going for the singularity."

The attendants had stopped when I'd whipped out the wand, frowning, worried it was a weapon. Worried they might be the targets.

There was an inarticulate roar from the top of the pyramid, inarticulate but not a whit unclear on its meaning, and the attendants were galvanized into rushing me, drawing their sidearms.

I drew my sword and shrieked to make them hesitate— and then leapt at the nearest and ran him through. "Bob"

146

blasted the other with an ozone-reeking bolt of blue-white lightning. "Bob"'s target went spinning, smoking, to fall in a blackened heap in front of the confused crowd. Stang dragged "Bob" to the partial cover of a corner of the pyramid and snapped off suppressive fire at the attendants.

I ran toward that great stinking, slobbering mouth, wand in one hand and sword in the other.

Some things are best not remembered. Some things you don't want to think about at all.

Never mind the details. The mouth was slippery and I could feel muscles rolling under its mucous membranes around me as I staggered toward the pulsing glow of the singularity stuck like an otherworldly tonsil in the flesh and tried not to let myself be distracted by vomiting from the carrion-stink of the long-dead, tried not to think about the bits of flesh underfoot, the carpet of human parts—and suddenly I was close enough. The wand was pulling the singularity from its place.

Almost. It almost came free. But its captivating field was itself captivated by the flesh of the Boss. It resisted.

And then the walls closed in. He was closing his jaws. I felt their crushing power, felt I was about to become one with the torn and rotting shreds of humanity on the floor . . . And soon one with the shit in his intestines. I was in deep shit already.

I turned my sword so it met the jaws as they came; it was propped between them.

The boss screamed—which sent a hurricane of stink into my face. But, gagging, I held my ground and thrust the wand through the dimness at the singularity. And now it tore loose, was sucked into the wand.

The Boss bellowed in frustration and loss and ground his jaws, disregarding the pain, so that my sword was pressed out of place. I grabbed it and turned, leaped for the open air.

And fell short. Fell on my face in the rot in a stinking creek of saliva as the jaws closed around me . . .

I looked up and saw the Boss's mouth closing, locking me into darkness. Out there, beyond those grisly lips, I could see Stang standing with his legs apart, both hands on the gun, aiming upward at something.

Then there was only darkness and fetid humidity and the crushing jaws.

BLAM. Stang's gun going off.

A rush of cool air and light as the boss roared, opening his mouth and jaws long enough for me to get to my feet and leap free, rolling out into the blessed open air, still holding the wand and sword.

I got to my feet and turned, saw that Stang had put a .44 slug through the Boss's forehead. Blown out his filthy brains.

The great pyramid quaked and began to split apart, gushing blood and oil and spitting sparks; the huge mouth vomiting a wet jigsaw of festering human parts.

The attendants were blinking in confusion, without their psychic enslavement; the new inductees were screaming, clawing the goggles off. The TVs had gone blank. Men and women ran in every direction, panicked, adding panic to panic to make pandemonium.

"Bob" was smiling broadly, puffing his pipe, hands in his pockets as he sauntered toward the door. He was humming, "The Battle Hymn of the Republic."

Stang and I followed. Stang wrinkled his nose at me. "Wheee-ewwwww, boy, you reek to high Heaven!"

"Good," I muttered. "I hope Heaven gets the message. Some things I saw today make me wonder what the hell God is up to."

In minutes we were out on the streets, and in the pow-der-blue Mustang convertible. Stang made me sit on an old newspaper. "I don't like rotting bits of human flesh stuck to my upholstery. Just a little quirk I've got."

"Oh I don't know," "Bob" said cheerfully. "Might be nice!"

Before I sat on the newspaper I read an ad on it.

HALFLIGHT HOMES. The HALFLIGHT develop-
ment on the planet JA-LUR will offer luxurious ten-
family homes for people looking for a SOOTHING
atmosphere, perpetual twilight and perpetual convenience! Pools, spas, lobe-retuners, cerebral-pleasure-
center interfacers, neurological video hookup, heated
waterbeds, AC, W/W Carpets, spacious kitchenettes,
pseudoterraces, quasitrees. Retire in fully com-
puterized comfort at . . . HALFLIGHT HOMES.
800,000,000 units planned. Put in your deposit now!
Priced to Sell! Contact *Outfit Realty, Unlimited.*

I sat my damp, sticky rump down on the paper and
hoped I soaked it through.

Stang started the car as I looked around. I was expecting
to see the place crumbling in on itself, maybe collapse
around us. But all that happened was that the residents
were either wandering around dazedly, not sure how
they'd gotten there . . . or were lying in broken heaps on
the ground, having fallen from overhead. The gravity trick
had failed when I stole the singularity.

My stomach wrenched at the sight. I hadn't anticipated
that.

But I steeled myself with one unimpeachable convic-
tion: They were better off. Better off dead and broken than
enslaved to the thing that had held them.

And I had freed more than I had hurt.

I clung to that, as we drove out of town. Out into the
dour, arid plains of the Darkland.

I watched the town recede behind us. It was a dizzying
construction, an angular, out-spiraling cluster like an ugly
Mandelbrot set; it refused to coalesce for the eye. It didn't
collapse. It just stayed and stayed, as such places always
do. It would grow shabbier and shabbier, more and more
stylistically outdated, but still it would stay; bits of it
would crumble in time, but overall it would remain intact,

getting grimy, accumulating a wealth of tackiness with each passing minute . . . but still it would stay. It would be deserted. Animals would nest in it. Dust and sand would cover much of it. But still it would stay.

I saw something else back there. Another vehicle. A three-wheeled black van with polarized windows, following us down the highway.

As I watched, it sped up to overtake us. It drew up parallel to us, and a window rolled down.

It was Draco. He had a rocket launcher in his hand. He grinned at us. Not pleasantly.

"Bob" grinned back at him. "Nice rocket launcher! You selling those? I could retail some of them for you!" He shouted over the noise of the engines.

Draco blinked in puzzlement, then shrugged, and aimed the rocket launcher at the front of our car.

Stang hit the brakes. The launcher fired.

The rocket hit the asphalt road just in front of us. The blast kicked the front end of the Mustang around to the right, and sent us spinning off into the plain. We skidded up on two wheels—and almost overturned. There was a distant, bemused look on "Bob"'s face. Luck was with us—because "Bob" was with us. We didn't turn over.

The car fell back onto four wheels, but the engine was out for the count. Automotively K.O'd.

The van had come around and was pulling up in front of us. Draco had put the rocket launcher aside. There was something meaner looking in his hand.

It was an industrial strength weapon. An autoblaster.

And it was pointed at me.

XIV

"I could probably move a few thousand of those blasters for you," "Bob" said, stuffing frop into his pipe. His grin didn't waver.

Draco blinked and shook his head. "Crazy bastards. Glad you snuffed that cocksucker pyramid dude, though. He had my brain in his pocket. He was gumming up the Big Plan."

"He was bringing the Outfit's life-style to Ja-Lur," I pointed out.

"Not with us in control, he wasn't. Makes all the difference who's in charge. Now, I'm gonna need that wand from you."

Stang drew his gun. "Forget it, pimple-eyes."

"Drop the gun, Slim Shim," Buckfinster said, stepping into view with another blaster in his hand. Pointed at Stang.

"You guys know my friends here by name, Draco?" I said.

"Know 'em by reputation. I said drop the gun, Slim, or we fry you."

Stang just glared at him. Draco raised the blaster. Stang cocked the pistol.

I said hastily, "If you know their reps, Draco, you know that they're dangerous. And not human, exactly."

"Yeah?" Draco chuckled. "What are they going to do? We got the drop on 'em."

Stang's eyes suddenly went sort of distant, as if he was thinking of something else entirely. He stuck his gun back in his coat and went to the trunk of the car. Draco pointed the blaster—but didn't pull the trigger, and I could see by the frustration in his expression it was because I was in the line of fire, and he didn't want to damage the containment field in the wand.

Stang opened the trunk, pulled a six pack of beer from a cooler, and tossed one to "Bob." He opened a can of beer, drank off half of it, belched, then began to roll a frop cigarette from a little baggy of the sacred herb, humming to himself all the while. It was a tune I didn't know.

"Bob" had finished his beer in one long swallow. He smiled at the empty can. "Beer. We ought to market our own brand of beer, Stang. *Slackmeister Beer*."

Draco was getting madder and madder. Buckfinster was quietly cursing us. He looked badly disheveled, which was for him the torment of the damned.

I maneuvered to stay between Draco and Stang. Draco pointed the blaster at my head. "Hand me the wand or I'll burn your head off."

"Okay," I said. "Here." I lifted the wand as if about to hand it over—but held it in front of my head. "You burn my head, you burn the wand. You'll destroy the singularity containment field. You burn me lower, I'll smash the wand as I fall. You burn my friends I'll smash it on the ground."

"You wouldn't do that."

"Try me."

Meanwhile, "Bob" and Stang had decided to ignore the situation. They sat on the rear fender of the Mustang, drinking beer and smoking frop. "We could buy up some generic beer," Stang said, "then relabel it *Slackmeister*."

"Not bad," "Bob" said, expelling excited chugs of frop smoke around the pipe. "Except for the *buying up* part. There ought to be some way we could con somebody else into putting up the capital outlay."

"I'm warning you bunch of lunatics!" Draco barked. He took a step toward me.

I raised the wand as if about to smash it. "Ah ah ah!"

He hesitated, then turned and got into a whispered conference with Buckfinster.

I looked at "Bob" and Stang—and noticed something strange. The smoke from their frop was forming itself into murky but recognizable shapes. The shapes of demons, twisting and curling in the air; demons made of smoke. Just glance at it, and all you'd see is smoke. But look closely and the demons became visible, the smoke curling into their shapes as if by chance. The faces of the horned demons drifting up from "Bob"'s pipe all vaguely resembled "Bob"; Stang's smoke demons vaguely resembled Stang. A diabolic Stang with pointed ears and horns.

The smoke demons drifted, unnoticed, over Draco and Buckfinster.

Somehow, Stang and "Bob" were invoking these demons—by goofing off. It was as if their idleness were a kind of ritual invocation in itself.

The smoke curled around Draco and Buckfinster, who took no notice of it. Instead, Buckfinster nodded at Draco and moved off to my right, while Draco moved off to my left, intent on getting me between them . . .

And then the smoke demons coiled themselves tight around their victims.

Draco and Buckfinster shouted, one low-pitched and the other high, and dropped their weapons to struggle with the ghostly bonds that formed around them. The smoke demons grinned at them in diabolic mockeries of "Bob"'s expression. Grinned and laughed in their faces. Draco and Buckfinster were tied up in laughing ectoplasm.

"Nice trick," I said admiringly.

"Takes years of practice," Stang said casually, crushing a beer can between his hands. He put it in the trunk of the car. He doesn't believe in littering, either.

"We should've snuffed 'em," Stang complained.

"Just doesn't seem sporting to kill unarmed men," I said. "How long will the smoke hold them?"

"About an hour," Stang said.

"We took their blasters and set the van on fire, anyway," I pointed out. "They're going to be slow catching up to me."

"Draco's probably got a way to signal for help on him," Stang muttered, shrugging. "You haven't heard the last of him."

Stang had tinkered the engine into starting and we were driving down the dirt road. The asphalt had ended a mile before. At its end we'd found a single lone gas station, the most outlying manifestation of the singularity's fantasy of the Outfit. The gas station was deserted, but the gas pumps worked. Restrooms worked too. I cleaned up, handwashed my clothes, and ate somebody's abandoned sandwiches from a Rambo lunchbox we found sitting on the desk in the filling station office.

Now we had a full tank of gas and lots of open road and we were barreling along at eighty, with the top up to keep the dust off us.

It wasn't enough. I had to get to the Darklord *fast*.

I asked, not for the first time, "You can conjure the Fightin' Jesus, you can conjure the laughing ectoplasmic fropsmoke demons, but you can't get us an interdimensional transport to the Darklord?"

"Stop whining," Stang said irritably, "I told you, this isn't our planet, there's all this supernatural activity we haven't got control of here. It's like using alternating current when you're supposed to use direct current. We're Alternating, this place is direct. We brought some of our own power with us—and we've used up most of it. Got to recharge. Or, if we get sick of this gig we could let ourselves get killed. That's a viable option too."

"Get *killed*?"

"If we get killed, all that happens is we go back to Earth, remanifest there, and our contract with the Darklord is over. But that's only half pay. No benefits, no overtime."

"So let's contact the Darklord and ask him to—"

154

"Already tried that," Stang said. "His line's busy. Concentrating on something else."

Later I was to learn that the Darklord was occupied repelling a full-scale attack from the forces of Sartoris. The Outfit couldn't send off-world troops to openly attack the Darklord. Not that Sartoris wouldn't turn hypocrite and use the technology and the people he despised to gain control of the planet; he would, assuring himself that he would discard the tool once the job was done. But he didn't dare take that step for another reason: The Unity would learn of it and step in. They were neutral where native Ja-Lurian conflicts were concerned—when outworlders were involved, the Unity would be involved. But I conjectured that Sartoris knew that if the Outfit could deliver the singularity to him, he could use it to destroy the Darklord with what would *appear* to be magic.

That afternoon, we drove hard for the Dark Spire, unaware that we were driving straight toward the outer edges of a full-scale supernatural battle.

The dim sun (not a variety of Chinese food) of Ja-Lur was sinking listlessly toward the horizon as we drove into a region of stunted, twisted trees, white stretches of salt, scratchy brush, occasional outbreaks of black sand dunes. We were deep in the Darklands.

In the far distance we saw thin columns of smoke rising, and flashes of light as if from distant lightning. I sensed it then, the supernatural battle raging just over that horizon; now and then I glimpsed ragged-edged spirits flying away from the battle, fleeing overhead from the bodies they'd left lifeless in the mud, looking like ethereal kites without strings . . .

"Bad scene over there," Stang said, squinting against frop smoke as he peered into the distance. "Not sure I want to party with 'em."

"Won't have to!" "Bob" said happily.

He pointed at the sky behind us. Something was hurtling through it, still a long way off.

"Heat-seeking missile," Stang said. "Draco must've signaled the Outfit some way . . ."

I nodded. It figured. Draco had the Outfit send it after us. No one gets the singularity if they don't.

I could make it out now. An elongated bullet silhouette against one of the rising moons. Coming right at us.

"It's homing in on the car, I figure," Stang said. He stopped the car, and dragged me out of the car by the wrist.

"Hey! We gotta—" I began.

But Stang had kicked me in the belly. I doubled over, gasping. He spun me around, and kicked me in the ass. I tumbled head first into the ditch. I heard the whine of the approaching missile as I got to my feet, turned in time to see Stang burning rubber, roaring away, leaving me out here . . .

And drawing the missile off. It rocketed past me, pursuing the car.

"Jump! Get out of the car!" I yelled, though there was no way they could hear me from here.

And then the missile caught up with the car. Struck the trunk of the powder blue '66 Mustang, which vanished in a ball of fire. I threw myself down as shrapnel whizzed past me.

After a few moments I got up, my gut aching for more reasons than the punch I'd taken, and ran up to the burning wreckage.

Not much left. Bits of car.

No bits of people, though. No bodies. Nothing. I watched the smoke curl up from the blackened metal in the crater.

I thought I saw faces in the smoke. "Bob" and Stang, mouthing "Good-bye!" Actually, Stang mouthed "Take 'er easy, buddy!" But it was good-bye.

If we get killed, all that happens is we go back to Earth, remanifest there.

I smiled and saluted. And then I set off on foot for the Dark Spire.

156

*   *   *

There's something about it in the Bible. The Bible from Earth, I mean. Jehovah is P.O.'d at Satan for tempting Adam into eating the apple, so he turns Satan into a snake and says he has to go about on his belly henceforth. Like it's a real insult to him or something.

But the Serpentines don't see it that way. They regard it as an honor to be snugged to the breast of the planet; they view it as the ultimate in grace, in bondedness, and think of people who go about on two legs as awkward and pretentious and neurotically isolated from the planetary consciousness.

The Serpentines are a very select tribe of Darklanders who worship serpents, and who, via magic, are part serpent themselves.

I knew them immediately as they came sliding toward me over the sand, moving as smoothly as any snake, the special muscles on their bellies and chests and arms and the tops of their thighs, supernaturally enhanced, rippling, drawing them along the ground . . .

And yet they are men and women (flat-chested women), men and women with scales and slitted golden eyes to be sure, men and women with darting tongues, Darklander men and women . . . but men and women nonetheless.

The whole tribe was there, heading Northeast, following their glossy-black, red-striped leader, their hairless heads moving sinuously just over the ground as they surrounded me.

"Kamus of Kadizhar," their leader said. "Your visit is inopportune." Her voice was as sibilant as might be expected. Exaggerated *S*s. *You* know the sort of thing.

"I'm on my way to the Dark Spire, Luce. You had to run from your warrens?"

Luce hissed angrily. "We are loyal to the Darklord, so the creatures of Sartoris sent their angry parts down into our warrens and drove us to seek refuge in foreign places. These are terrible creatures, Kamus. They appear to be demons—but they are worse. They are machines!"

157

I had to smile. There is a Luddite streak in the Serpentines. In all Darklanders, really.

But the situation was no laughing matter. It looked as if Sartoris was taking technological help from the Outfit after all—but disguising it as some organic supernatural monstrosity to throw off the Unity.

I wondered how much good it would do to report it to the Unity. Each side in a war is prone to accusing the other of the use of forbidden weapons; nerve gas, biological warfare, torture. The Unity would be skeptical.

Luce's head moved sinuously from side to side as she recollected her people's ordeal. "They are creatures taller than you, Kamus, who like you have the regrettable penchant for standing upright. But when attacked they break up into little machines that enter our burrows and harry us. They killed one of my daughters, and one of my husbands." Luce's tongue flickered over my ankle, tasting me. A gesture of friendliness. "Come with us away from this place, Kamus, and I will take from you the burden of walking upright. I will invoke the Crawling Goddess, and give you sleekness, and horizontal passage, and you will become one of us. If you play your cards right, perhaps I'll marry you. I'm short a husband now. We could fertilize some interesting eggs together."

"That's a tempting offer," I said, trying to fake sincerity. "But I have to go on. I'm on a Mission for Jann-Togah."

"You will not reach him. You will only encounter the Soulless, who have driven us into the terrible agoraphobia that is the great world. The Soulless are the paradox of Sartoris. He preaches Darklander purity. He preaches Darkland fundamentalism. He promises an end to modern things, to off-worlders, to the plague of their technology. But the Soulless are made by his off-world allies—the Goddess told me this—and they are machines, inside themselves. They have no taste, these Soulless ones, no feeling for the Darkland. Could they see a phosphorescence rising from a swamp and know its beauty? Could they see the poetry in a dead tree, the murderous elegance in a spider-lizard? Do they appreciate the varieties of ground cover, or the esthetic rules of protective coloration? Could they know the sacred communion of swallowing a rat alive? Can they revel in the glory of a stroke of lightning, or the excellence of the varieties of darkness? Probably they think darkness is darkness and have no notion of its fine gradations. What do they know of the delicious character of foul weather? The austere glory of a drought? They are Soulless. They have no taste."

"They sound like real drips," I said. "I'll try to avoid them. Where were they when you last saw them?"

"Not far behind, and virtually everywhere. I wish you luck, and bid you good-bye."

"Good-bye, Luce. Good luck to you and your tribe."

They slithered away to the northeast, looking like the detached shadows of men wandering off on their own. They moved quickly, in graceful slaloms, over the hill and out of sight.

I pondered my situation. It didn't look good.

Maybe I'd better try to get the Darklord on the psychic line. I chanted the appropriate chant—and waited for the Darklord to reply.

All I got was a psychic recording. "Sorry, Jann-Togah is occupied with matters of state just now. But if you'll leave a message after the queasy sensation, I'll get back to you."

I left a message and broke the connection. I looked around, thinking I could perhaps comandeer another kragor. None were within mindcasting distance. There was only the sinister, intermittent shivering in the ground from explosions somewhere up ahead of me. And up ahead, too, were the Soulless.

I wanted to turn and follow Luce.

I thought about Andalaya. I trudged onward, toward the Dark Spire.

More than once in my life, I've felt like I'd wandered behind enemy lines without knowing it. Only I hadn't, not really.

Not till now.

One moment I was alone, wandering down a sere, stony ravine, the next they were there, surrounding me. They'd descended from the sky in the blink of an eye. The Soulless ones.

I drew the blaster and searched my mind for an appropriate spell. Nothing occurred to me. My mind was a blank. I hate it when that happens.

They were each twice my height, and, as Luce indicated, they were Soulless. I could sense their hollowness. They were great leathery Standard Devils, with bristling horns and barbed fangs, seven red eyes apiece all the way around their heads, long whipping reptilian tails; the hind legs of dragons and the arms of giants, ending in razor-sharp talons.

You know the sort of thing.

"I don't buy it!" I yelled. "I know you're not demons, you're too damn generic for that and anyway I've had a tip-off on you! You're machines! Controlled by someone from the Outfit! Transmit this to him: Back off or I'll report you to the Unity! I've got a communicator on me, I can call them anytime I want!"

I doubted they'd believe that particular lie, but I was desperate.

The largest of the Soulless ones, on whose head a flame flickered to make him seem more terrible, leaped down into the ravine and stood in front of me. "Give over the wand, Kamus of Kadizhar, and you will live!" it boomed. Obviously an electronic voice.

"Kiss my ass!" I replied, and blasted him pointblank with the raygun.

He exploded into ten parts, and all the ten parts came at me, each alive unto itself, and each one intent on killing me.

XV

I'm not a bad shot with a blaster. I had to use it more than once on Bronze and elsewhere, before I came back to Ja-Lur. And this was kind of like skeet-shooting.

The robot demon had exploded into parts that whirled around me, the clawed hands grabbing at me, the legs and feet kicking at me, the torso splitting up into two segments that together formed metal-toothed jaws in the air, the head flashing by, snapping at me, the tail split into two parts lengthwise, trying to whip around me. I blasted the arms and legs with four quick, accurate shots, ducked the tails, shot the head right between the eyes as it came screaming at me. It split into two parts that came at me from opposite sides. I blasted those and sidestepped the torso-jaws and ducked the tails again, shot them as they went by—and then the other Soulless were there, jumping down around me and charging.

I had less than one second to decide what to do.

I pressed the blaster to the containment globe on the wand, and shouted, "Stop right where you are or I'll destroy it!"

They stopped. Right where they were.

The arms and legs of their chieftain froze in place, in midair. The head had come back together and was glaring at me from its hovering place.

"The ensuing explosion would kill you, too," it pointed out.

"You'll kill me anyway," I said. "And I'd rather destroy the singularity than have it fall into your boss's hands." It was a logic I knew they understood. A little heat-seeking missile told me so.

"What do you expect us to do? We cannot retreat. It is not in our programming."

"Communicate with your boss. Tell him to tell you to lay off."

"I am communicating with the Programmers . . . They say 'Give him one more chance to hand it over, and if he doesn't play ball, kill him and the Hell with it.'"

"That's one way we could go with this thing," I conceded. "But there's another option." I adjusted the knob on the blaster to tight focus. I aimed it carefully at a corner of the wand's globe . . .

Okay, right: I was taking a chance. I was taking a chance as big as space is wide. I knew it probably wouldn't work. But I didn't have a lot of options just then. I had two options: certain death and probable death. Guess which one I chose.

I fired the blaster. A needlethin bolt of energy sliced out, and sheered off a piece of the globe. I hadn't destroyed it—but I'd intentionally ruptured it.

I had damaged the singularity containment field.

All its myriad possibilities began to leak out—and I focused my will on them through the Tenth Level of Visualization, using the Raja disciplines I'd learned as a young warlock.

The robotic demons lunged at me.

And struck a transparent steel wall. I had erected the wall with the instantaneity of thinking about it. I thought transparent steel wall—or pictured one, anyway—and one appeared.

Nice. I could learn to like this.

They battered at me on the other side of the enclosing sphere of glass. I laughed at them and pictured the sphere

splitting into segments that slapped downward and outward, over the Soulless ones.

It happened. The transparent steel segments smashed
them down and then enclosed the Soulless ones in small
globes. They were locked in, and would remain so—until
Sartoris or the Outfit set them free. I decided not to allow
that. I focused my mind on the quantum singularity leak,
and the transparent steel globes constricted, very suddenly,
to the size of beachballs. The self-reconstructing gizmos
inside them couldn't reconstruct from dust. The spheres
shuddered and became motionless. I held up the wand,
focusing, and was lifted into the air by a golden dais that
formed beneath me out of the rock at my feet. I made it
gem-encrusted just for good measure.

It carried me up, high into the sky, across the wasteland
of the Mordant Plains . . . and out over the battlefield. I
could see the barren, ravaged battlefield through rents in
the black smoke; could make out dark figures two hundred
meters or more below, the silver uniforms of the
Darklord's minions and the flat black of Sartoris's people.
Silver and black, in places splashed with red. On both
sides of the crater-pocked plain were the demons, real and
mechanical, who were these armies' equivalents of tanks
and artillery. They flung balls of jet and argent flame at
one another that exploded on the giants' mindshields—or,
as often, among the men around them, blasting more cra-
ters and sending men flying like scarecrows in a wind-
storm. I saw a golden giant twenty times the height of a
man, a giant with reptilian wings on his head, with eyes
that gave out green sparks, and blue fire for teeth, thunder-
ing out across the battlefield, leading a thousand men in a
charge; the men firing arrows that they directed mentally
to their targets, swinging enchanted swords edged in fluorescent silver flames. The golden giant who fought for the
Darklord was met by a great four-headed black dragon that
wrapped its long necks around its antagonist and squeezed
like a family of giant pythons. The golden giant shook the
world with a roar and bit into a scaly neck and *burned*

through it, so that sizzling ichor rained on the hapless men below; they shriveled under it and screamed. Other rebels nearby met the onrushing Darklord army, arrow for arrow and sword for sword, magical weapons that rarely missed their mark; losses on both sides came quickly and in great numbers . . . Freed souls fairly gushed up from the battlefield, rising like a cloud of sentient steam from a volcano . . . The slaughter was terrible to behold, but still the armies came, reinforcements on reinforcements, wave after wave, the black and silver charging one another over the heaped-up bodies of their fallen comrades, plunging head-on into mutual decimation, their bodies sprawled against the ground abstracted by death to resemble random numbers scattered on a dark page, mocking the cruel statistics, statistics printed in crimson . . .

I was sickened by the sight and drew myself higher into the sky so as to make it all less personal. From up here it was almost a wargame board.

Sartoris was gaining ground, a double phalanx of Soulless robot demons driving the loyalists back, exploding when struck by demonic lightning bolts, each exploded robot becoming a dozen smaller horrors twice as virulent.

Such tactics were brutally unfair, but before the Unity could intervene, it would be all over. The Darklord would succumb. And Sartoris would hide the evidence.

But the Darklord had one hope. One he had perhaps given up on.

Me. Kamus had arrived and had tapped into a great power source. The power to bend reality.

I was giddy with the energy at my fingertips. How to use it? How to channel it best? Against whom? Numberless possibilities presented themselves . . .

Perhaps I could simply wish the battle over, with no more loss of life and the Darklord the victor. But some insistent hunch warned me that this would require an outpouring of too much reality-shifting energy. I wouldn't be able to control it. I just couldn't command an event so large: I couldn't visualize it perfectly enough. But there were other ways.

I gathered a storm around me.

The power is all there, in the atmosphere. Or, indeed, on the ground. In a clod of dirt—perfectly ordinary, non-radioactive farmer's dirt—is a planet-busting subatomic energy, locked away but seething with potential.

The power was easier to find, in the air. It was there in electrical charge, in air pressure and humidity, in the brooding of clouds. I focused on the wand, and through it reached out, gathered the storm in my arms—and flung it.

The clouds grew out of seeming nothingness, a clot of mist becoming a great roiling mass of cumulonimbus, the color of gray silk dusted with charcoal. It boiled around me like the hurricane around the eye, flashing in pockets of light here and there, making crooked-dagger jabs of lightning, electrons striking in twisty streams of electricity outward from me . . .

From *me*! I laughed in joy and wonder and delight. Me! *I* was the focal point of all this power, and the thrill of it roared through me like a hundred years of sexual lust compressed into ten seconds. Shivering with pleasure, I *fired* that thrill downward, in the form of a great fist of wind and rain power, a fist studded with lightning like brass knuckles, which *smashed* into the ground in a breach between the two armies, then *burst* outward, sending raging winds to either side, flinging the two armies apart from one another, and the dragon away from the giant. I sent a particularly large bolt of lightning to fry the multiheaded dragon, leaving something that resembled charred campfire hot dogs; several more giant bolts downed the other Sartoris giants.

I conjured tornados out of the howling storms and sent them to snatch up the Soulless ones. They were carried out over the horizon and dropped in the sea in blocks of instant stone.

Sartoris's army, seeing whose side this Olympian storm was on, turned and took to its heels, demoralized.

I pursued them, directing the storm from my little open-air flying saucer, having criminal amounts of fun, for a good half hour.

Then I skimmed my craft directly to the fortress of Sartoris himself.

Originally, Sartoris had been a local baron, and the castle had been a crumbling artifact belonging to his ancient family. As he accrued followers, he accreted the supernatural power that came with their allegience and used it to build up the fortress into something that bespoke a young and vibrant ambition.

At the center of the fortress was the old castle, your standard black-stone castle, textured with age, with battlements, with towers and slit windows, with its own chapel (for worshipping the Elder Gods), with a courtyard and stables. No garage, or carport; no swimming pool or jacuzzi.

It looked old; sections of stone were missing and the stained-glass figures of Ba-al and the Yacatisma were short some panes. Around the castle were the glassy, dark green walls of the new fortress, like a monstrous windowless bunker hundreds of meters to a side. Its only distinguishing feature was a single onyx obelisk, carved with runes, thrusting up from a smooth roof like an antique antenna. Over the whole thing was a faint translucent blue glamour I knew to be a sorcerous shield against attack.

As I approached the fortress a ruby-red bolt of energy the size of a starship fired from the tip of the obelisk and hurtled toward me. It was enough power to melt a small moon. I almost let myself be intimidated. If I had, I'd have been nonexistent in a second. Even my soul would have been incinerated.

I focused, and the energies in the wand created a hand out of the dust and moisture in the air, a great transparent gray hand that caught the red bolt like a baseball and flung

166

it back at the obelisk. It struck the shield—which shivered and collapsed; the outer walls of the fortress cracked . . . but held.

I had to be careful, I reminded myself. Andalaya was in there, somewhere.

I raised the wand . . .

The Darklord stood beside me on the flying dais.

He was there and he wasn't. It was a projection of some kind, I judged from its tenuous outlines. But the projection looked mad.

The dark figure of Jann-Togah pointed at me and bellowed, "Fool! Stop this childish tinkering! Bring the wand to me and let me handle this! You don't know what you're doing! You haven't the knowledge to handle this power!"

"I'm getting her out, and I'm getting her out *now*!" I snapped. "I can handle this! I was born for it!"

Born for it? As I turned my attention back to the fortress, I wondered what I'd meant by that.

A scythe was slicing through the air toward me; Sartoris had taken advantage of my distraction. It was a steel scythe blade big as the sail of a ship, slicing horizontally toward me, in the hands of the hooded figure of Death himself. *"I have come for you, Kamus!"* skull-faced Death announced, in a voice that comandeered all of the authority of a starry night.

Sartoris was trying to freak me out.

I visualized, focused, and the scythe fragmented before it reached me, breaking up into little bullet shapes that went flying back through the image of Death—who simply vanished. I sent the hail of bullets back to the obelisk, smashing into it, chipping away some of its crucial runes.

I amplified my voice so that it matched Death's, and thundered, "Give her over to me unharmed, Sartoris! Now! Or I'll think you into oblivion!"

That was an exaggeration. The singularities trapped in the wand didn't exactly grant wishes. You had to visualize the thing just right, you had to work with the matter and energy near at hand, and there was a certain amount of resistance from the background. Certainly, Sartoris would use his psychic force to resist any attempt to simply make him vanish. He'd feel it coming.

I waited alone on the hovering platform, the wind whistling around me. Feeling Sartoris pondering my threat; waiting for his reply.

I looked for the Darklord, but he had gone. I knew he was watching, somewhere.

"She comes to you, Kamus." The voice of Sartoris, whispering in my ear as if he stood invisibly beside me. I jumped a little, then chided myself for falling for that one.

A trapdoor opened in the roof of the fortress, at the base of the obelisk. Andalaya floated out the trapdoor, into view. She was supine, floating like the tranced assistant in a magician's levitation trick, her eyes closed and her hair trailing below her. She floated up toward me, limp, and I was sure he had killed her, was delivering her corpse.

But then she was deposited on my flying platform, at my feet. I touched her, and reached out with my Darklander intuition to be sure it was truly her. Sartoris might be foisting a supernatural fake on me.

No. It was Andalaya. Alive and unhurt. She was in suspended animation.

My hand trembled near her cheek—but I didn't touch her. Best if she didn't wake until the fight was over.

I heard Jann-Togah's voice, out of the air, "Look out, you fool!"

I looked up and screamed. My nightmare was coming to get me.

It's a nightmare I have, from time to time. The first man I killed. His name was Regnos, and he was drunk, and he hated Darklanders, and he came at me with a sword and a blood oath . . .

I was young then. Later I realized it was quite possible I didn't have to kill him. He was sluggish; I could have sidestepped him, knocked him out perhaps. There were ways. At the time I reacted in anger and instinct. I could have . . .

Maybe not. Maybe I couldn't take the chance. Maybe he'd have killed me if I hadn't killed him. I don't know.

Regnos had come to represent for me my horror of the necessity of killing. Not of the act of killing itself—but the fact that I am *forced* to kill sometimes. The ugly necessity. And the nagging fear that I might be a murderer with a ready bag of rationalizations. Always wondering, every time it was necessary, if there might have been another way . . .

The thing flying toward me had the body of an Earth vulture and the head of Regnos. The rotting, sword-cloven face of Regnos shrieking its accusation at me, spitting blood with the words. It dropped down at me, claws extended.

I cringed—and it grabbed at the wand in my hand. I jerked the wand reflexively back, fighting my horror as Regnos thrust his rotting face close to mine, screaming, "Murderer! Murderer! *Murderer!*"

I closed my eyes—and Regnos's face shoved itself through the darkness behind my eyelids, as if that darkness were thin black tissue. His exposed brains, split skull cloven by my sword, dripping blood on my cheeks as he screamed, "MURDERER!"

I visualized, focused, and the face became papier-mâché that blew up into confetti and floated away.

Gasping, I sat up. The headless vulture was flopping around on the platform like a chicken with its head cut off, slashing the air with its talons all too close to Andalaya. I disintegrated it with a wave of the wand, and, still sick with emotional uproar, got to my feet.

Sartoris had used my distraction with Andalaya to attack me—and now he'd used my distraction with the Regnos vulture to launch another attack. This one struck home. The platform erupted beneath me.

I never knew what he used to shoot it out from under me. But suddenly the thing had exploded under my feet, was in fragments around me as I fell.

I was falling through a flock of Regnos birds, little ones

the size of blackbirds with tiny little bloody heads, flying at my face and shrieking, hundreds of little bloody man/birds screeching "Murderer, Murderer!" and clawing at me—

Enraged now, I made a great sweeping motion with my arm and cooked them all into headless, plucked squabs that fell out of the sky . . . a strange rain, one for Charles Fort . . . And then I was in freefall. I used the wand to stop myself, and Andalaya, falling near me, and collected a flying ship of ice around us.

And the ice ship began to crack, to fall apart.

It wasn't Sartoris's doing. It was mine.

I had imagined what Sartoris might do next and in my furious concentration had done it myself. I pictured the ship whole again and so it became—but then a great hammer, big as a clock tower, came swinging out of the sky at me. And that, too, was my own creation.

I averted the hammer and sent it spinning toward the obelisk of Sartoris. But then Andalaya was up, standing beside herself. There were two Andalayas, one on the ice, asleep, one standing and pointing at me, shouting in a voice that was at once Regnos's voice and her own, "Murderer! You killed my brother! You killed Hojas!"

The guilt I had suppressed since Hojas's death came searing up in me like hot bile, and I couldn't control my thoughts, couldn't keep them from working with the wand to create . . . myself, standing beside Andalaya, staring at me with contempt.

Drawing my sword and coming toward me.

Raising the sword. To punish me. For murder.

Murdering myself as punishment for murder. The sword gleaming overhead . . .

"No!" It came out of me with a primal urgency as I raised the wand and blasted myself—the false image of myself I'd conjured up—into mist. The mist swirled over the false Andalaya and carried her away into nothingness.

But no sooner were they gone than Hojas was there, lying on the icy deck, dying again, whispering that he just wanted to be someone else, someone better . . . just wanted . . . wanted to be . . .

I used the wand to dispel the false Hojas—but the pain of seeing him remained in me.

I felt Sartoris, somewhere nearby, poised to take advantage of my confusion.

I didn't care. I had blundered, I had killed, I had failed.

In that moment I saw my life as a series of blunders culminating in the accidental killing of the brother of the woman I loved. I saw my clumsy tinkering with events at the Outfit town, and the dissolution of the gravity trick, the broken, bleeding bodies in the street afterwards.

There are two ways to look at your life. I looked at mine through a lens darkly. Maybe it was Sartoris's influence. Maybe it was Regnos and the accusing look in the fake Andalaya's eyes. Maybe it was the truth. Despair closed around me.

I surrendered. I waited for death.

171

XVI

And then the realization hit me. My death in this place meant Andalaya's death.

I threw up a hasty shield, and a bolt of black lightning rebounded from it. I willed the ship into retreating, back toward the Dark Spire.

The Darklord was right. I couldn't control this thing. It had affected me first with megalomania, then had slid its secret fingers into the recesses of my unconscious, a connection perhaps triggered by the Regnos apparition Sartoris had cunningly sent. I had been unable to control my own will, my own creativity.

I had to retreat from the conflict, from the stress and distraction of it, and focus on one thing. Getting to the Dark Spire. I couldn't defeat Sartoris alone.

I ran, I sailed toward the Dark Spire in my sleek, translucent ship of silver-blue ice, leaving a wake in the clouds. I made a warm bed of silky furs for Andalaya and stood beside her, glancing at her sleeping face from time to time as I guided the ship. Unable to bring myself to wake her. I could not face her accusation, yet.

But the fight with Sartoris wasn't over. He just isn't the kind of guy to let an affront slide off his back. He holds grudges.

Sartoris pursued me with an emerald sea serpent who swam the clouds around the ship as a serpent swims the ocean, dipping and surfacing and dipping again, rearing up and feinting toward me, trying to draw off my energies. Sartoris sensed I was growing weary and couldn't guide the ship and fight the sea serpent, too. It waited till my fatigue was a great weight on me—and then it attacked, rearing up out of the cloud in front of me, hissing gigantically, its eyes spearing out poisonous rays of green, its emerald coils rippling back the dull iron of the sunlight.

I hesitated and knew I was lost. Screwed. Fucked.

And then a meteor arced down from the heavens, burning like Greek fire, and crashed into the serpent, sending it burning and hissing and dying to the ground far below.

"Now hasten back to me!" The Darklord's voice. It was he who'd called the meteor down from space.

I reduced the ship to a fast skiff and hurtled it faster through the air to the Dark Spire.

"Take it from me," I said. Some part of me rebelled and wanted to hold onto the singularity wand; felt that giving it up was giving up some supernatural manifestation of my masculinity. But I fought down that part of me and placed the wand in Jann-Togah's hands. "You were right. I was out of my head on the stuff."

As soon as I gave it to him, I regretted it. I didn't regret not keeping it for myself. I regretted not turning it over to some authority at the Unity.

Because now all that power was in the Darklord's hands. How would he use it?

I'd wanted to be rid of the thing as quickly as possible, to keep myself from doing harm with it. But, as usual, I was dogged by irony. By handing the wand over to the Darklord, I might have condemned the world to an ironclad dictatorship.

The Darklord took the wand into the tower; through the open door I saw him place it, rather gingerly, on an altar. With a gesture he enclosed it in a protective bubble of quivering black. "I hope that holds it," he muttered, as he returned to me.

We were out on the upper cupola of the Dark Spire, a slim black tower rising like a lonely skyscraper from the wastes of the Darklands. The balcony was a thing of slick black stone inlaid with silver filigree. A living gargoyle, squat and tusked, perched on the rail of the balcony, standing guard; it filed one of its daggerlike teeth with a rasp. It was humming "I am the Walrus," and it nearly was.

I poured myself a glass of bloodred wine from a decanter on a golden table, and stood sipping it, looking at the peacefully sleeping face of Andalaya, laid out beside the table in her bed of furs.

"Why not wake her?" Jann-Togah asked, rather distantly. He wasn't really interested.

"I'm going to do that, after I have a drink," I said, a trifle defensively.

He went to the rim of the balcony and looked out over his domain. Smoke still rose in a desultory way from the battlefield, where a brushfire burned, but the battle was over, at least for now.

The gargoyle sang, sotto voce, something about yellow matter custard.

I glanced through the open door at the altar, wondering if I should try to take the wand back, deliver it to the authorities. I'd never be able to break the protective bubble alone. And it was likely that the Darklord would kill me for trying. I was his ally, tentatively, and not his friend.

He didn't have any friends. He didn't want any friends. They were a liability.

I looked again at Andalaya. What was it Francis Bacon had said? Something like, "A man who takes a wife gives hostages to fortune." Fortune and I had nearly got her killed. And I'd killed her brother, indirectly.

I swallowed another long draught of the wine, and my own culpability. Both burned on their way down.

But dammit, I'd been trying to save a world. Three great and foolish forces had been wrestling for Ja-Lur, like children fighting over an egg. One of them would have dropped it.

I don't know if it was the wine, or the logic. Both could be heady. Whatever it was, I was beginning to feel better. I had done what I had to, to the best of my abilities, and flawed as they might be they were all the gods had given me.

I set the wine goblet aside, bent over, and spoke the words that would break the spell of suspended animation.

Her eyelids fluttered. She opened her eyes and winced. She whispered something hoarsely, something I couldn't make out. I bent nearer and she repeated it.

"Aspirin . . . aspirin and coffee, for pity's sake . . ."

We sat at a glass table on the balcony, drinking coffee imported from thousands of light years away. Each cup cost as much as a successful merchant earns in a month. Andalaya had had hers free from Hojas; now she was getting it from his great rival. We drank it from china cups poured from a wrought-silver service, also imported from thousands of light years away.

Andalaya sat beside me. She was neither friendly nor unfriendly. She dipped a croissant in her coffee and chewed it mechanically, staring gloomily over the balcony rim at the river Ja-Kanak, which flowed like listless ink into the base of the tower, far below.

"I'm surprised you show such restraint with the wand, frankly," I remarked, passing the Darklord the sugar. "I expected you to use it immediately against Sartoris."

He put two lumps in his coffee and stirred it, frowning. "Your clumsy modification of the field with the blaster has damaged it. It has become unstable. Dangerous. I have erected a second field, but I'm not sure it will hold it."

I glanced nervously at the doorway. "Should we really be hanging around, waiting to see?"

"I can go nowhere," Jann-Togah said, "until I have made a decision or two. There is much to reckon."

"Maybe I could help you figure it," I said, "if you'd tell me the truth about what's been going on."

He shot me a hard look. Of course, all of his looks are hard. Usually they're like getting a slingshot pebble between the eyes. This one was more like a chunk of steel from a catapult. "What's all this?"

"There's too much that doesn't add up. First Buckfinster pretends to try to talk me into quitting the job and leaving the planet. That was bogus right there. And you think I don't know you've got agents at the spaceport? People on the lookout for any energy source that comes in that might be dangerous to you? You'd know instantly if someone brought a black hole to Ja-Lur. You wouldn't be likely to let it slip through your fingers. You'd sure as hell know if it was being set up on top of one of your own mountain ranges. And then there was Buckfinster again—sometimes acting like a bumbler, sometimes as efficient as a Unity agent. Like he was being directed from somewhere . . . It didn't add up."

Jann-Togah nodded his head, just once. "Truly, you are the Darkworld Detective." He clapped his hands and shouted something to a servant. The servant bowed and scurried off, returning minutes later with . . .

"Buckfinster!" I said. Not really as surprised as I sounded. I knew it had to be him. He was the one common denominator, besides me, that had drawn the singularity to Ja-Lur and the Darklord.

He tipped his plumed hat. He was cleaned up and sartorially resplendent once more. The expression on his face was irritatingly smug. "You have found me out, it seems."

"You're an agent for the Darklord?"

"All along, as you have evidently surmised. When Jann-Togah heard that the Outfit had stolen the Black Hole of Carcosa, he sent me to make contact and to try to channel it here. He knew they were making plans to use it to exploit Ja-Lur. And he knew that Sartoris was about to become a serious threat." He shrugged, sat down at the

176

table, and poured himself some coffee. "I had to pretend to try to dissuade you from the job, as part of my cover."

"And you were going to subvert Sartoris and friends in some way on that mountaintop so that Jann-Togah could steal the singularity to use against Sartoris . . . and the Outfit?"

"Right. We were going to steal the cannon the Outfit had provided, as well. Hojas was a blind, a bit of protective coloration to keep Sartoris from seeing the hand of the Darklord. If he got out of hand, the Darklord would have killed him. Which he nearly did. But the explosion of the cannon killed him instead . . . You were the X-factor in the equation, Kamus. So the Darklord decided to take you into his employ . . ."

Andalaya was glaring at the Darklord. He ignored her. The gargoyle moved closer to him, keeping a baleful yellow eye on Andalaya. The gargoyle was singing, softly, "The Fool on the Hill."

"You had the singularity—why not just give it to Jann-Togah?" I asked, though I had already guessed the answer.

"I *didn't* have it. The Outfit had it, and they guarded it with all their power. Their technological power is equivalent to the Darklord's supernatural power. But enforcing an antitechnology mandate with sorcery would have destroyed the singularity's containment field. So we had to get the singularity another way. The Darklord picked Hojas as the unwitting intermediary. The Outfit were convinced they could control Hojas. So was the Darklord. But he was harder to control than anticipated."

"Especially after the Outfit involved Sartoris in their plot against me," the Darklord said. "Things very nearly got out of hand, when we lost the singularity on the mountaintop." He seemed faintly amused. "But Buckfinster has worked for me for a long time, and he was quite capable."

I looked at Buckfinster in amazement. "You really *are* Zorro. You were very believable, when you and Draco ran the Mustang off the road . . ."

"I was planning to take the wand from you, and deliver it—and Draco—to the Darklord. Draco could be useful to us . . . I wouldn't have killed you in the process, unless it was absolutely necessary. I just had to have the wand— frankly, I was sure your luck had run out, and you'd lose the wand to Sartoris before you could deliver it yourself. Draco is a dangerous man—and capable of signaling his associates at any time. I had to play the game with him a while longer. Believe me, I prevented Draco from killing you more than once. Unfortunately I was unable to prevent his calling that missile down from the Outfit's orbital platform."

Jann-Togah looked at Buckfinster. "Did you take care of that matter?"

Buckfinster nodded. He looked at a timepiece, and then at the sky. "The bomb on the shuttle should have reached the platform just about . . ."

In the dark sky, high overhead, there was a wink of light. Something very big, but very far away, exploding.

I shuddered. How many men had died on that platform, in that instant, as the Darklord calmly buttered his croissant?

The Darklord nodded in satisfaction. "I will give you a bonus this month."

"Perhaps you should recruit Kamus permanently," Buckfinster suggested. "After things fell apart on the mountaintop, he did very well. Recovered all three singularities. Saved my life, by accident, after I had rather carelessly fallen under the spell of the boss . . ."

I shook my head, disgusted. "I don't need to be part of any more byzantine plots, knowingly or unknowingly. I'd rather use my own foot for shark bait."

"What's a shark?" Buckfinster asked.

"Never mind," I said. I was looking at Andalaya. She was gazing fixedly at a butter knife on the table. She looked at the knife, and then at the Darklord. I hoped she didn't try it. It wasn't sharp enough to hurt him, but he would take the attempt seriously anyway.

Buckfinster looked at the Darklord and asked softly, "Did you weaken the, ah. . . ?"

The Darklord nodded curtly. He looked expectantly at the door to the room containing the wand. In moments, his expectations were realized.

Draco stepped out onto the balcony, with the wand in his hand.

He brandished it, "No one gets in my way, see, or I smash this thing here and now . . . and we all go up in smoke!"

The wand looked as if it was in fact ready to "go up" in some way. It was pulsing with all the colors of the rainbow, humming nastily.

The gargoyle tensed, about to spring at Draco. But the Darklord raised a hand. "No. Don't try to stop him, Paul."

The gargoyle sat back on its haunches, shrugging. It began to sing, softly, "Being for the Benefit of Mr. Kite."

It had a rather nice tenor, actually.

Draco was edging toward the rail of the balcony, keeping the table between him and the gargoyle. He looked expectantly at the sky.

"You expecting a helicopter?" I asked.

"Naw, wiseguy. Sartoris sprang me from that hick jail cell down there and he's gonna get me outta here . . . Yeahhhhh, there it is."

There it was. A djinn riding a blue tornado. A fat djinn with cockroaches for eyes and a tendency to snigger obscenely. As the whirlwind approached, napkins and bread crumbs were blown off the table. The djinn swept down to the balcony and caught Draco—complete with the wand—up in his arms. I nearly made a grab for the wand, but a look of warning in the Darklord's eyes restrained me.

Laughing, Draco and the djinn whirled away through the air, in the direction of Sartoris's fortress. Draco's voice was heard faintly over the tornado, "So long, suckers."

The Darklord chuckled at that.

The djinn vanished with Draco and the wand. I stared at the Darklord. "You had him prisoner here. . . ?"

"Yes. Buckfinster rendered him unconscious and brought him here."

"And then you let him escape?"

"Sartoris sent some invisible spirits snooping around after the wand, as I knew he would. I allowed them to slip through my defenses and I lured them to Draco's cell. Allowed them to release him, and allowed them to direct him to the wand."

"And you weakened the protective bubble over the wand—"

"So the spirits could damp it down long enough for Draco to steal the wand. Yes."

"You *want* him to have the wand . . ."

"I do now. When you brought it back I saw that it had been damaged, was becoming unstable, was about to reach critical mass and explode. Or implode, as the case may be. It will not destroy the planet. It will merely destroy an area about . . . well, let us see for ourselves."

He spoke Language and gestured significantly, and a dusky oval mirror appeared before us, over the table. Its interior shimmered and produced shapes. It was a sort of supernatural telescope, and through it we could see the fortress of Sartoris, as the djinn descended on it with Draco and the wand. The trapdoor opened at the base of the obelisk. The djinn descended through it, carrying his precious charges. The trapdoor closed.

"Maybe you timed it wrong," I said. "Maybe he managed to stop the—"

I broke off, as a quivering ball of dark violet energy billowed up around the fortress. The fortress convulsed and collapsed in on itself, cracking down the middle and sucking itself into the crack. In seconds, the fortress and the ancient castle were gone, imploded, pulverized and compressed and drawn down into nothingness . . . Leaving only a wide, smoking crack in barren ground . . .

And then a geyser of rainbow fire rose from the crack, spouting upward toward space itself. A great sword of burning colors penetrating from the ground to the upper atmosphere.

The Darklord pointed a finger at the mirror, and his face was rigid with concentration. A crackling black fire issued from his finger and penetrated the mirror; far away, it surrounded the gap in the ground where the fortress had been, and then coalesced around the base of the tower of multicolored flame. The polychromatic geyser, prompted by the Darklord, propelled itself skyward like a spaceship taking off. It rocketed into the sky and was gone.

"Hopefully, if I've calculated things right," the Darklord said, "the deteriorating singularity will miss the moons and the sun. Will return to Carcosa. It's much too unstable to exploit effectively hereabouts . . ."

He poured a little brandy into his coffee. His hand was shaking, just slightly. But he was pleased with himself.

"You didn't know for sure you could control that reaction," I said. Accusingly.

He looked at me blankly. "It might have gone awry. But it didn't and now Sartoris and most of his followers and a number of very annoying people from the Outfit are gone." He snapped his fingers, and the mirror vanished.

"You could have blown up the damn planet," I objected. "You were risking millions of lives."

"Only on this plane of existence. Anyway, it's better Ja-Lur not exist than for it to be ruled by that callow slug of an upstart."

I shook my head in wonder. "Power is a sickness."

"Oh *do* stop being so self-righteous, Kamus, dear fellow," Buckfinster said, helping himself to the brandy.

"What about the Outfit?" I asked, hoping to rain on the Darklord's parade. "Most of their local representatives are still around, in Mariyad."

The Darklord cracked his knuckles meditatively. "I will

have the others removed when I show the Unity the Soul-less Ones I have captured—they broke the Unity laws by introducing forbidden weaponry to the local 'primitives.' The Unity will bar the Outfit's people from the planet.''

"They'll be back," I said. "And what about the war? Rool and Hestia and Adelan, the Stinking Hordes—they're all about to go to war."

"That was the doing of Sartoris," the Darklord said. "Stupid. Unnecessary violence is a waste of resources. With his malevolent influence gone—and nothing else to distract me—it should be a simple matter for me to diffuse the war. I'll simply liquidate a few over-ambitious would-be conquerors.''

I was watching Andalaya from the corner of my eye. Her left hand was sliding under the table toward an ornamental dagger on Buckfinster's jeweled belt.

She made her move—and I made mine.

I grabbed her wrist as she grabbed the hilt of the knife. I wrenched her away from him, and took the dagger. She fought me; we tumbled backwards off the chairs.

Jann-Togah looked at her and spoke a few words in Language.

She went limp. Her eyes closed. She stopped breathing.

I stood up, looking at him, feeling the dagger in my hand. Thinking I was going to kill him myself.

He read the look on my face and smiled. "She's not dead. Just 'suspended,' as she was before. You can awaken her after you take her away with you."

I relaxed a little and dropped the knife.

"I really should kill her," Jann-Togah went on musingly, "because she wants to kill *me*. She's not likely to find a way, but you never know. However—you have served me well. As a bonus to you, she may live."

"Great. Fine. Screw this gig. You mind if we leave now? Can we go back to Mariyad?"

He nodded and made a languid gesture at the gargoyle and a clucking noise. The gargoyle seemed to understand perfectly. It drew a horn from a pouch on its belly and blew in it.

From around the back of the Spire came a black limousine.

A long black limo with a red leather interior. It was floating in the air. It had no wheels, but apart from that and the fact that it could fly, it was an ordinary and very comfortable-looking limo. It waited at the edge of the balcony. I picked Andalaya up in my arms. No mean feat. She's a big girl. I approached the limo.

The gargoyle went to the passenger's door, opened it for us, singing that the Magical Mystery Tour was coming to take us away . . .

The office looked the same as when I left it. Dust. Vermin trails. Insects specking the window. Bad smell.

I opened the window, put my phonecub on the new desk, sat behind it, fed the phonecub a sweetmeat, and wondered what to do next. Mission accomplished. Ja-Lur safe for now. The Outfit—the Conspiracy, Stang had called it—vanquished, at least for the time being. I ought to feel good.

But I felt the way my office looked. Maybe a new coat of paint. On the office, not on me.

After I'd dropped Andalaya off at her place, with a spell set to waken her after I left, I'd gone to report to Captain Sark, and then Staurian. He was well satisfied and paid me off, and the money was heavy in my pockets. It was a weight that threatened to pull me down through the floor.

I stood up, drawing my sword.

Someone was trying the doorknob.

I padded across the room, yanked the door open.

It was Andalaya. She had my battered hat in her hands. She looked tired but beautiful. "You forgot your hat," she said. "Left it at my place when you dropped me back there. Insible wanted to give it to a hound-troll to sniff you down with." She smiled wanly.

I sheathed my sword. "Thanks." I took the hat awkwardly. "I'd invite you in—but the place is pretty shabby just now. How about a drink somewhere instead?"

"I can't."

"Sure. I knew that. I'm sorry about what happened, Andalaya. I was trying to, uh—"

"I know. You were trying to save the world. Hojas was doomed anyway. It was obvious, from what the Darklord said. Thanks for coming to get me from Sartoris."

I cleared my throat. "Sure. Sure."

"But . . . I feel kind of . . . kind of used up, after all that happened, Kamus. I can't see anyone right now."

Especially, I thought, not someone who had killed her brother. I said the inevitable two words. "I understand."

"But listen—come over to the place sometime for one on the house. Any girl you choose."

"Any?" I asked, looking her in the eyes. "Any but the one I want?"

She shrugged, and there was a flicker of mischief in her eyes. "Give it time—and we'll see." She came into the office just far enough to kiss me, once, quickly. She looked around the office and made a face. "I see what you mean."

Then she left.

Feeling a little better, the money a little lighter in my pockets, I went to my desk and sat down. Found a stale stick of juicy fruit in a drawer and chewed it till it wasn't so bad anymore.